THE UNICORN TREASURY

THE UNICORN TREASURY

Compiled and Edited
by Bruce Coville
Illustrated by Tim Hildebrandt

 A DOUBLEDAY BOOK FOR YOUNG READERS

A Doubleday Book for Young Readers
Published by Delacorte Press
Bantam Doubleday Dell Publishing Group, Inc.
666 Fifth Avenue
New York, New York 10103
Doubleday and the portrayal of an anchor with a dolphin
are trademarks of
Bantam Doubleday Dell Publishing Group, Inc.

ACKNOWLEDGMENTS

"The Lore of the Unicorn" copyright © 1987 by Bruce Coville.
"The Unicorn in the Maze" copyright © 1987 by Megan Lindholm.
"Unicorn" copyright © 1957 by William Jay Smith. Used by permission of the author.
"A Net to Catch the Wind," by Margaret Greaves. Copyright © 1979 by Margaret Greaves. Reprinted by permission of Harper & Row, Publishers, Inc.
"Riddle" copyright © 1987 by Myra Cohn Livingston.
Excerpts from A Swiftly Tilting Planet, by Madeleine L'Engle, copyright © 1987 by Crosswicks, Ltd. Reprinted by permission of Farrar, Straus & Giroux, Inc.
"Ragged John" copyright © 1987 by Bruce Coville.
"Homeward Bound" copyright © 1987 by Bruce Coville.
"The Paint Box" first appeared in The Flattered Flying Fish and Other Poems, by E. V. Rieu. Copyright © 1962 by E. V. Rieu.
Chapters 14, 15 and 16 from The Transfigured Hart, by Jane Yolen. Originally published by Thomas Y. Crowell. Copyright © 1975 by Jane Yolen. Reprinted by permission of Harper & Row, Publishers, Inc.
"The Unicorn," by Ella Young, first appeared in the March 1939 issue of The Horn Book Magazine. Used by permission of The Horn Book, Inc.
"The Snow White Pony" copyright © 1987 by Ardath Mayhar.
"What News the Eagle Brought," from The Last Battle. Copyright © 1956 by C. S. Lewis. Used by permission of the Estate of C. S. Lewis.
"Unicorn," by Nicholas Stuart Gray. Reprinted by permission of Faber and Faber, Ltd., from Grimbold's Other World, by Nicholas Stuart Gray. Copyright © 1963.
"The Princess, the Cat, and the Unicorn" copyright © 1987 by Patricia C. Wrede.
"Starhorn" copyright © 1987 by Shirley Rousseau Murphy.
"The Court of the Summer King" copyright © 1987 by Jennifer Roberson.
"The Strangers," by Audrey Alexandra Brown. First printed in Challenge to Time and Death (Macmillan of Canada). Copyright © 1947 by Audrey Alexandra Brown.
"The Boy Who Drew Unicorns" copyright © 1987 by Jane Yolen. Used by permission of the author's agent, Curtis Brown, Ltd.

Library of Congress Cataloging-in-Publication Data
Coville, Bruce,
The unicorn treasury.
Summary: A collection of stories, poems, and unicorn
lore about the mythical creature.
1. Unicorns—Juvenile literature. [1. Unicorns.
2. Animals, Mythical] I. Hildebrandt, Tim. ill.
II. Title.
GR830.U6C68   1988   398.2'454   86-32919
ISBN 0-385-24000-7
ISBN 0-385-41930-9 (pbk.)

3 5 7 9 10 8 6 4 2

For Diane

B.C.

CONTENTS

THE LORE OF THE UNICORN

by BRUCE COVILLE

What is a unicorn?

At first glance the answer may seem so obvious that the question itself is silly. Everyone knows that a unicorn is a horse with a horn stuck in the middle of its forehead.

Right?

Well, yes—and no. The answer is much more complicated, and considerably more interesting, than that.

What unicorns actually do look like has been a matter of some dispute for several centuries now. Some old accounts give them white bodies and red heads, with a short, three-colored horn. Others give them elephant's feet, a boar's tail and other equally improbable traits.

Oddly, while writers continued to disagree over what unicorns look like, artists kept coming back to the same basic idea: an animal much like a horse, but (in the better pictures) lighter and more graceful, with many goat-like qualities. In particular you should expect a unicorn to have a silky beard and hooves that are split, or cloven, like those of a goat.

But even though we can describe a unicorn as having some of the traits of both these animals, in truth these creatures are far more magical than either a goat or horse could ever hope to be. Even the best descriptions fall far short of what you would see if you actually met a unicorn some moonlit night beneath an apple tree. (Not a bad place to look, by the way. Some unicorns are wisdom personified, and wisdom can, indeed, often be found beneath an apple tree on such a night.)

Unicorns have many strange abilities. But of all the things they can do, it seems we are most fascinated by their power to heal. For the touch of a unicorn's horn can pull us away from death, toward immortality.

Unfortunately for the unicorn, the horn retains its power even without a unicorn attached—which has led people to hunt it rather ferociously.

The basic method for catching a unicorn is fairly simple. A pure young woman is taken into the woods and placed beneath a tree. Since unicorns are irresistibly attracted to such young ladies, if there is a unicorn in the vicinity it will come and lay its head in this maiden's lap. At this point she may sing to it, or slip a golden bridle over its head.

Once the unicorn has been tamed in this manner, the hunters leap out from hiding and either capture or slaughter the beast. When they do, the greatest prize, of course, is the horn itself. (Though some people also believe there is a precious jewel, a "carbuncle," hidden underneath the horn.)

The correct term for the horn is "alicorn," a word some people think was invented simply because "unicorn horn" sounds so awkward.

Alicorns are among the most powerful of magical items. They were prized by popes and kings because they provided protection against all manner of evil, including epilepsy, pestilence and poisoning. A horn set in the middle of a table would begin to sweat, or form a dew, if any of the foodstuffs had been poisoned. Even a little powder filed from such a horn was an antidote to the most toxic substances. Small wonder that in a place like fourteenth-century Italy, where poisoning was a common way to deal with one's enemies, these horns were considered treasures indeed.

As might be expected, an item both so valuable (horns sometimes sold for ten times their weight in gold) and so rare (some legends have it that there is never more than one unicorn on earth at a time) was a great temptation for frauds.

With so many people selling false alicorns, it was necessary to find a way to determine which were real. Some of the tests included:

* Drawing a ring on the floor with the alicorn. A spider placed in such a ring would not be able to cross the line, and in fact would starve to death trapped within the circle.

* Placing the horn in water, which would cause the water to bubble and seem as if it were boiling, even though it remained cold.

* Placing a piece of silk upon a burning coal, and then laying the horn on top of the silk. If the horn was truly an alicorn, the silk would not be burned.

* Bringing the horn near a poisonous plant or animal, which would burst and die in reaction to it.

The trade in alicorns was very real in the Middle Ages, and many noble houses listed one of the mystical horns among its treasures.

However most of us today would agree it is far better to leave a unicorn's horn where it belongs: on top of its head!

With its horn properly in place, a unicorn can do many wonderful things. One of the most well known is purifying water for other animals, a trick known as "water conning." Generally this takes place where there is some venomous animal haunting the water hole. The serpent, or whatever, will slip out at night and poison the water. But at dawn the unicorn comes and dips its horn in the pool. Immediately the water is clean and pure once more.

Three famous warriors have been connected with unicorns—Julius Caesar, Alexander the Great and Genghis Khan. Caesar's connection was minor; he wrote of a unicorn that lived in the Hercynian Forest. But of Alexander it is actually said that he rode a unicorn—the famous Bucephalus, who many think was only a horse, but others claim was a unicorn. (Considering the fame Bucephalus gained as a war-horse, he was probably a relative of the kar-ka-dann, which you will meet below.) It is also said that Alexander and his men once had a battle with a tribe of unicorns. As for Genghis Khan, it is written that in the year 1206 he set out with a great army to conquer India. As he was standing in a mountain pass overlooking that great country, a one-horned beast came running up to him and knelt three times in token of reverence. The Mighty Khan took this as a signal from his dead father, and turned his army back.

Clearly, unicorns are known the world over. In addition to the horned horse-like/goat-like creature we are familiar with, there is the Chinese unicorn, called the K'i-lin, which had a multi-colored body and (some said) a horn twelve feet long.

K'i-lin was very special to the Chinese. It was a creature of great power and wisdom, and its appearance was always a sign of good fortune. The most famous example happened over 2,500 years ago, when the K'i-lin came to a young woman named Yen Chen-tsai. Into her hand it dropped a tablet made of jade, the beautiful green stone used in much Chinese art. On the stone was a message, prophesying that she would become the mother of a "throneless king."

The prophecy was true, for Yen Chen-tsai became the

mother of the great Chinese sage Confucius. Confucius never wore a crown or commanded men. Yet his teachings did as much to shape China as the power of many kings and warlords combined.

It was said that K'i-lin walked so softly its hooves made no sound. Some believed that this was because it was so soft-hearted it did not want to crush the blades of grass beneath its feet. It had a voice like a thousand wind chimes, avoided fighting at all costs and lived for a thousand years.

How different was the unicorn of Persia, the fierce and ferocious kar-ka-dann, a terrible beast that could attack and kill even an elephant! The only thing that could tame this savage animal was the ringdove; so soothing did the kar-ka-dann find their gentle calls, that it would lie peacefully beneath a tree where they were singing for hours on end. Though other animals couldn't even graze in the kar-ka-dann's territory, the ringdove was actually allowed to perch on the beast's horn.

Despite its worldwide fame, there are those who believe there are no more unicorns. One reason people give for their disappearance is that when Noah built the Ark, the unicorns didn't make it on board, either because they were too large, or too silly—playing games and frisking about until Noah couldn't wait any longer.

Others think they were simply hunted into extinction.

Still others believe that the unicorns left when the world became less sympathetic to the old magic, fleeing to some-place better suited to their strange beauty.

Saddest of all are those who believe there never were any unicorns to begin with.

Where did they come from, where have they gone, were they ever here at all?

The truth is, no one knows for certain.

But here's what I believe: wherever else they may have come from, unicorns live inside the true believer's heart.

Which means that as long as we can dream, there will be unicorns.

THE UNICORN IN THE MAZE

by MEGAN LINDHOLM

In the city called Grand lived a boy named Willem. The city was fabled for its tall crystal spires, for its shops full of rare merchandise and for its good and beautiful Princess. But Willem was too busy searching the ground for lost coins to notice the spires, he never had money to buy from the fancy shops and the Princess Morena didn't know he existed, much less care. Willem was a street boy.

He was not respectable. He wore dirty rags, and his bare feet were always splashed with mud. He didn't get much to eat, so he was smaller than other boys his age, and thinner. His hair was uncombed, and his face was dirty. He earned his living in nasty ways. He stood outside taverns and sang rude songs, to make the drinking men laugh and throw coins. He stole fruit from the fruit carts, and cooling bread from behind the bakery. He picked coins from people's pockets, and locks came unlocked under his fingers. He was nasty and suspicious, and no one liked him.

Except Agatha. Agatha was a potter who lived in the forest at the city's edge. A bubbling spring fed the stream that flowed past her cottage. She dug clay from the stream banks, softened it with the spring's water and turned it into pots on her wheel. She once told Willem that her spring used to be a unicorn's spring. Once folk came to it from far and near; some to drink of its curing waters, some hoping for a glimpse of the unicorn. The unicorn, she said, was a marvelous beast, shining with honor, wisdom and strength.

Just to see him strengthened the soul. But others came also, hunters who wished to kill the unicorn for his magical horn. Yet he always managed to escape them and return to his spring.

Then one day Princess Morena rode past the spring. Her goodness and beauty were so great that the unicorn followed Princess Morena back to her palace to live with her forever. The King had a wondrous maze built, and there he had hidden the unicorn, safe always from the hunters. Now only Princess Morena and her mute handmaiden knew the way through the maze to the unicorn and the curing water he touched with his horn. Now he wore a jeweled halter and ate the finest foods. His old spring was only a place of cool water and green grass.

Agatha had told Willem that story when he was very sick. A pastry vendor had caught him stealing an apple tart from his cart, and had given Willem a terrible beating. Willem had barely been able to crawl away into an alley. There Agatha had found him when she came to town to sell her sturdy pots. She had loaded Willem up on her old donkey and taken him home to her cottage. She had nursed him until he was better, and then put him to work helping her dig clay and even showed him how to shape the red lumps into pots on her wheel. Willem had cared little for such work.

"Why," he asked her, "should I muck in mud all day, to make a pot worth a few pennies? I could steal that much in the wink of an eye!"

Agatha had shaken her head. "Willem, Willem. Stealing is wrong. Work honestly for your pennies. It's unkind to take someone else's."

Willem laughed. "Unkind? Why should I care? They've never been kind to me! They hold their noses when I pass, they chase me from their stores. Why should I be kind to them?"

"Be kind to them for kindness' sake or . . ." Agatha paused. "Or because if they catch you stealing again, they'll cut your hand off. Or worse. You've seen what they do to thieves in the Punishment Square. Do you want that to be you?"

"They'd never catch me!" Willem boasted. Still he shivered, remembering the thief who had been caught breaking into the unicorn's maze. The execution had been in the Punishment Square. The Royal Guards had thrown him into a cage with a tiger. A hungry tiger. Willem had watched, too horrified to look away. He still had nightmares about it. Yet that didn't stop him from running away from Agatha as soon as he was well. He didn't trust her kindness. "She only wants to get work out of me," he told himself.

Back to the city he went, to sing his nasty songs on corners, stealing coins and bread. Still, sometimes, on rainy nights, he went back to Agatha's cottage. She always let him in and gave him a bowl of hot soup. But she also scolded him for his wild ways, and if he wanted to sleep by her fire, he had to first study his letters. Willem saw no sense in letters; he did it only to earn his place by the fire. Agatha knew that as soon as the weather turned warm again, Willem would return to the city.

He liked his wild life. He had no chores or lessons. He was free to hang about the city gates, greeting the rich caravans and sometimes guiding a wealthy noble to the palace for a few coins. People came from distant kingdoms, their horses laden with treasure, to buy the tiny flasks of unicorn water that the Princess sold. Poor people also came to the city gates, but Willem didn't guide them to the palace. They had no pennies for him, and he knew that they would get no unicorn water. The unicorn water was very costly. Not a single drop was ever given away, no matter how one begged. Sometimes Willem felt sorry for the people who came so far to beg water and were turned away. But there was nothing he could do to help them.

Occasionally, Willem would visit Agatha in the market where she sold her pots. She'd ask what he'd been doing, and if he'd been earning pennies as a guide, she would be pleased. When he had been idling and stealing, she would sadly scold him. After a while, he just didn't visit her on his stealing days. Sometimes many days passed without Agatha seeing him.

One cold and windy day, Willem decided to visit Agatha. "Maybe I can load her unsold pots and lead her donkey home. Then she'll give me a bowl of soup. And I can sleep by her fire, after I study those silly letters." But Agatha wasn't at the market square. "Perhaps," he thought, "Agatha didn't come to market today. I'll go to her cottage."

Her little donkey brayed when he saw Willem, kicking up such a fuss that Willem went to his pen. The poor beast had neither food nor drink. "That's odd," thought Willem as he fetched hay and water for it. "Agatha never leaves her donkey hungry or thirsty." He knocked on her cottage door. There was no answer. Willem pushed the door open.

Agatha lay on the floor, too sick to move.

Willem put her to bed, and fetched cool water from the spring for her. Then he cooked her some soup, and tidied the cottage. Dust was thick on the table and the clay dry on her wheel. Agatha had been sick for many days. "If I had not come today," Willem thought to himself, "perhaps she would have died, all alone out here!"

Agatha wouldn't even try to eat the soup he made. "I am too sick," she whispered hoarsely. "And too old. I am going to die, Willem. When I do, I want you to have my cottage

and donkey and potter's wheel. Live an honest life, Willem, and I won't mind dying so much."

Those words bothered Willem much more than any of her scoldings. "Don't be silly," Willem told her. "We'll get you well, and you'll go on being a potter. And I'll go on being a thief."

"No." Agatha shook her head. "I've had this sickness before, when I was a little child. I nearly died then, but my father took me to the unicorn's spring. The water flowed silver, and I drank some and was cured. That was many years ago. Now the unicorn lives in a fancy maze, and wears a jeweled halter. There is no hope for me, Willem. My strength is gone. Please stay with me. I don't want to die alone."

"Silly talk!" Willem turned away so she wouldn't see his tears. "Did you think that I would let you die? No! I'll just nip off to the city and steal a flask of the unicorn's water. I'll be back before the sun rises."

"Please, Willem, don't!" begged Agatha. "It's hard enough to die alone! Don't make me die knowing you've gone to your death for me. Only Princess Morena knows the way through the maze. It has many a cunning trap to kill a thief. And if you survive the maze and are caught . . ." Agatha shuddered and coughed.

"I know, I know," said Willem. "Then it's into the tiger's cage for me!" He tried to sound carefree. "But I won't be caught, Agatha! I'm the slyest, swiftest thief in the city of Grand. Have no fear for me!" He put more wood on the fire and went out the door, heedless of her pleas.

Despite his bragging, Willem shook as he hurried toward the city. No thief had ever survived the terrible traps of the unicorn maze; the pits with sharp stakes in the bottom, the ponds of flesh-eating fish, the poisonous snakes, the great fanged beasts, the spring knives and choking vines. "Only the Princess and her mute handmaiden know the path to the unicorn." When Willem said that, a strange idea came to him.

Every evening, the Princess and her handmaiden were escorted from the palace by twenty Royal Guardsmen. The handmaid carried a little silver bucket and a brown wicker basket. The good and beautiful Princess Morena always wore a white silk gown with a golden sash. The Guardsmen marched around them until they came to the black gate that sealed the unicorn's maze. From there the Princess and the handmaid went on alone.

Willem began to run.

He reached the city without a moment to lose. The Princess and her handmaid were just coming down the palace's marble steps. Willem pushed through the watching crowd. Down a twisting alley he ran, up a side street, then up a rain barrel onto a roof, across five more roofs and then down an ivy trellis. He stood facing the barred iron gate to the unicorn maze.

The street was quiet. The gate bars were as thick as his wrist, and didn't rattle; they were too close together for him to slip between, and too stout to bend. The gate could withstand the strongest thief. But it hadn't been built to withstand a skinny boy. Willem lay down, his face in the dirt, and forced his head under the gate. The bottom of the gate scraped his ear and as he wriggled under it, his ragged shirt tore. But he was inside the unicorn maze. He heard the trumpets and marching feet that heralded the arrival of the Princess. The walls of the maze were formed by a prickly hedge thick with wicked thorns. Willem huddled like a hunted rabbit in their shelter. Crouching low, he held his breath and watched.

The Princess had arrived. From her golden sash she took a black key. The great gate swung open before her. The handmaid pushed it shut behind them and it locked with a loud clack. The Guardsmen turned away and sheathed their swords as the Princess entered the maze. They did not see the shadow that crept from the hedge to follow her.

The Princess Morena's white gown shone like a beacon as Willem hurried after it. And he did have to hurry, for the Princess lifted her skirts and strode rapidly as soon as she was out of sight of the people. Willem tried to keep track of the turnings they made, the lefts and rights, the statues and benches they passed, but in his rush to keep up with the Princess he soon lost track. He dared not follow her too closely, nor lag too far behind. Once he turned a corner and could not see her. His heart fell, but he heard a scolding voice and hastened toward it. It was the Princess.

"Oh, hurry up, Elsie, do! Tie your slipper later. I had to leave three handsome Princes to do this silly errand. I don't know why father insists I come. You know the way perfectly well and could go alone. But he says we must keep up appearances. Silly idea. The unicorn is mine. That's all that matters. Elsie, come along!"

Elsie rose from tying her slipper and went. And a small shadow followed, thinking that the Good and Beautiful Princess Morena was also a Nag. On they went, and on, through the twisting maze. Then suddenly the maze opened into a great square, with statues and benches of silver and marble. A fountain splashed high in the center. Willem ducked behind a bench. He heard a rustling and a rattling and several small thumps. The Princess spoke. "Hurry up, Elsie, I haven't got all night! And you—out of my way, you disgusting old thing." There was a splash as the handmaid filled her bucket, and then the rustle of the Princess' gown and the tap of her shoes. Willem waited until they were gone. Then he stood up.

He crept to the edge of the fountain's pool and stopped.

Agatha had been wrong. Willem saw no honor or wisdom or strength. He saw bony and mangy and old. The unicorn was the homeliest creature he had ever seen. The beast stared at him with red eyes, then lifted his horn and shook it angrily at Willem. Willem stared back, then laughed. "You can't get me!" he said boldly. "You're chained down."

And he was. A tiny bridge led to the unicorn's island in the fountain. Chains of black iron were locked tight just above each cloven hoof. He wore a halter of silver studded with jewels. An iron chain fastened him to the manger, and the weight of the halter kept his head bowed, so that the spray of the fountain landed on the glistening horn and dripped from there to a marble basin. "There," Willem thought. "That's the unicorn water!"

Over the slick stone bridge he crept, onto the unicorn's island. It was littered with rotten fruit, with a basketful of fresh spilled atop the old pieces in the manger. Willem hooked a peach from the top of the heap. "Seeing as how you don't care to eat it," he told the creature. The unicorn made an ugly sound and lunged awkwardly. Willem avoided him easily. The chains slowed him down.

The unicorn water in the marble trough shimmered silver. Willem stared at the water. Here he was, where no thief had ever stood before. Slyest of the sly was Willem, boldest of the bold. "And stupidest of the stupid!" Willem declared angrily, for he had nothing to fetch the water in. The ancient unicorn poked Willem with his spiraling horn. "Ouch! Get lost, you ugly old thing!" he cried angrily, shoving the beast away. With a sharp cry of pain, the unicorn staggered sideways, then slipped to his knees.

Willem looked down on him, torn between surprise and shame. He hadn't meant to hurt the creature. He remembered what it was like when the big boys pushed him down and kicked him because he was small and ragged. The uni-

corn looked up at him with eyes full of anger and pain. Willem understood those feelings. He knelt by the fallen animal, looking at the patchy coat and thin body. "They don't feed you right, do they?" he said softly. The cruel black chains had chafed the creature's legs raw. Exhausted with pain, he set his head down and the jewels in the silver halter rang against the bare hard stone. The unicorn shivered in the chilling mist from the fountain.

Willem was a thief and a liar, a teaser and a cheat. Yet he was also a boy who had been alone and hurt once, and received kindness from a stranger. Something turned over in his heart. He looked closely at the chains. "Huh!" he told the unicorn. "I've picked tougher locks than these. I'll have you free in half a minute."

It was not as easy as he thought. He had a bent pin, such as many a thief carried in the hem of his shirt. But the light was fading, and the captive didn't know the boy was a friend. The unicorn waved his horn feebly and kicked at Willem. When that failed to drive the boy away, the unicorn snapped and then swatted Willem in the face with his lion's tail. Still Willem worked doggedly on, until every slender leg was freed. The halter proved easier, for though it was chained to the trough, only heavy iron buckles held it to the unicorn's head. When it dropped away the old unicorn raised his head slowly, as if he found the sudden freedom strange. He rose and staggered away.

"Wait!" Willem called. "You don't know the way!"

But the unicorn did not understand what he said. He found a tussock of grass by a marble bench and nibbled it hungrily. "We have to get out of here!" Willem told him. "Do you want to be captured again?" The unicorn feinted at him with his horn, but was old and weak and Willem was fast as a pickpocket. He seized the slender horn and gripped it. "Come on," he said, and dragged the unicorn into the maze.

Evening had faded to night. In the darkness the maze was strange. "Did I turn here?" wondered Willem. "Have I seen that statue before?" And with every step, the unicorn backed and struggled. Once Willem took a wrong turning. He stumbled over a set wire, and an arrow whizzed above his head. Luckily the arrow had been set for an adult thief, not a boy like Willem. Back he went, tugging the weary unicorn along, until he was on the right path again. Once he heard a snuffling sound on the other side of the hedge, and then a growl. He hurried on, turning to the left, remembering that statue of Cupid, and that clump of thorny blossoms. At last they came to the great iron gate.

"As for me," Willem whispered, "I can wriggle under it. But what about you?"

With a sudden lunge the unicorn broke free. "No!" cried Willem, grabbing at his horn. "Come back here!" The creature dodged away from him, then suddenly paused. The unicorn looked at the gate that led to freedom, and at the small boy who seemed to block the way. His eyes grew bigger. The weariness in them changed suddenly to proud defiance. Slowly he straightened his spindly legs. He lifted his head high, and his thin neck arched proudly. "You can't do it," whispered Willem as he watched the beast gather his pitiful strength. "Please don't try!"

The unicorn leaped upward.

Willem had seen horses jump and goats frisk and deer bound. But never had he seen the leap of a unicorn. For an instant, the unicorn soared and was all Agatha had said he was, noble and wise and strong. Willem's heart rose in his throat as the unicorn cleared the gate.

Then the brave leap ended in a staggering crash. The

force of it drove the unicorn to his knees. He collapsed in the dusty street, the last of his strength spent. He lay still.

Under the gate went Willem, scraping his back and leaving skin behind. He knelt by the rickety old unicorn whose eyes were closed. Fearfully, he put his hand on the bony ribs. The unicorn half-opened his eyes and snorted weakly. "You dummy!" said the boy. "I'll have to help you."

The old unicorn had been starved and weighed little more than Agatha's donkey. But Willem was not a large, husky lad, only a skinny beggar-boy. Sweat stood on his forehead before he got the old unicorn to his feet. And that was only the beginning of the task. They staggered together down the dusky streets. At any moment, Willem expected to hear the shout of a city guard.

Out of the city they tottered, into the forest, and past Agatha's hut to her donkey's stall. The little donkey drew back in astonishment. Willem shook down straw to make a soft bed for the unicorn. There the creature sank to his knees. "I'll be right back!" Willem said.

Agatha's bucket lay by the water's edge. Willem snatched it up. "I'll dip his horn in this to make unicorn water to cure Agatha," he said as he filled the bucket. "Then I'll find him some sweet hay to eat. Poor old thing."

When Willem got to the stall with his bucket, the unicorn was gone. No sign remained of him except for a crushed place in the straw.

Willem had failed. Agatha would die. "This is what comes," he said bitterly, "of being kind. Agatha was kind to me, but I let her chance for life slip through my fingers. I was kind to that wretched beast, but he ran away from me. I should have pushed the ugly thing into the pond!" Yet even in his despair, his hands remembered the tingling warmth of the unicorn's body. He knelt to touch the spot where the creature had lain.

He went at last to sit by Agatha's bedside. There was nothing else he could do. She was so pale and worn that it hurt to look at her. Toward dawn, she woke. "Did you steal the unicorn's water?" she asked worriedly. Willem shook his head. Slowly he told her the whole story. Agatha listened, nodding now and then. He finished by saying, "And then the stupid old thing ran away."

Agatha smiled. She reached to touch his hand. "Willem," she said weakly. "Just because you help something, it doesn't mean you own it. Some things," she added, "have to keep their freedom, to keep on being what they are. Maybe the unicorn feared you were going to trap him. Be glad you helped him, for kindness' sake."

"He should have understood," Willem insisted angrily.

"Maybe, someday, he will," Agatha said comfortingly. Her hand fell back to her covers. "A drink of water, please," she asked. Her voice was fading. She would not last much longer. Willem took the bucket and went.

He tucked up his trousers and waded out into the stream to where the water was cool and clear. He dipped the bucket and watched the water run into it. Suddenly a strand of flowing silver twirled into the bucket, transforming the water into a shimmering mirror. Willem straightened slowly, saw the spring gleaming silver all around him. And just upstream . . .

He was still old and thin. The scars of the chains still marred his slender legs. But his coat gleamed clean and white and his head was lifted proud and free. An errant drop of water fell from the spiraling horn he lifted in salute to Willem. A shiver ran up Willem's spine. He lifted his hand in greeting, but the unicorn was already turning. With stately tread he moved away until his white shape was lost among the silver birch trees. When Willem looked down

again, the spring ran with ordinary water. But the water in his bucket shone silver with magic.

Agatha drank it. Two days later she was turning pots again. This time, Willem didn't run away back to the city. He never learned to read or how to turn pots. He did learn to recognize kindness, and found he had a talent for shaping clay with his hands. In years to come, many traders came from far away to buy his statues of unicorns. When they asked how he knew so well the shape of the beast, he would only look at his hands and smile.

As for the Good and Beautiful Princess Morena, without unicorn water to bathe her face every day, she became quite homely. She had to content herself with marrying an Earl's younger son rather than a handsome Prince. She went away with him, and the unicorn maze grew wild and unkempt. Even so, many folk still believed the unicorn lived there. Willem knew better, but he never told.

"If they think he's there," he said to Agatha one evening, "then they'll never go hunting him elsewhere." Then a thoughtful look crossed Willem's face. He looked at the clay unicorn he was shaping. "I wonder how he finally knew that I wasn't trying to trap him. What made him finally know I meant him kindness?"

"I wonder, too," Agatha agreed. But it was not the unicorn statue she looked at as she asked the question, but Willem.

UNICORN

The Unicorn with the long white horn
    Is beautiful and wild.
He gallops across the forest green
So quickly that he's seldom seen
Where Peacocks their blue feathers preen
    And strawberries grow wild.
He flees the hunter and the hounds,
Upon black earth his white hoof pounds,
Over cold mountain streams he bounds
    And comes to a meadow mild;
There, when he kneels to take his nap,
He lays his head in a lady's lap
    As gently as a child.

William Jay Smith

A NET TO CATCH THE WIND

by MARGARET GREAVES

It was high summer when Mirabelle first saw him. He was only a foal then, the color of gray moonlight, with a silver mane and tail.

She had slipped away from the palace into the deep forest beyond. Mirabelle loved the forest. It was cool and full of shadows and little shifting pools of sunlight. It was strange and secret, full of unknown things, magic things perhaps. It sheltered flocks of colored birds, and rabbits and squirrels and the big-eyed, delicate-footed deer. It breathed with the scent of flowers and the sound of running water, and at night it held all the stars in its branches.

The foal was grazing alone, fetlock deep in grass and flowers, in an open glade between the trees. He had not seen her. He was so beautiful that she hardly dared to breathe. Then the light wind took her scent toward him. He raised his head and lifted a curled foot, till with a startled whinny, he swerved and galloped away.

"Oh, don't go!" she called after him. "I'd never hurt you. Please don't go."

Perhaps he heard her. As he reached the trees he turned and looked back. Dark and round and shining, his eyes met hers, shy yet friendly, as if he understood.

When she returned to the palace Mirabelle told her father, the King, about all the things she had heard and seen in the forest. But she never said anything about the moonlight-colored foal. Her father boasted that he had the most magnificent horses in the world, and he could never see a fine one without wanting to own it. Mirabelle felt that her foal should never be owned. He was free as cloud and sky and water. So she said nothing at all about him, though day after day she longed for him and looked for him. But she never again glimpsed a single hair of his silver-gray coat.

Summer flowed softly into autumn. The leaf-ripping wind shrilled through the forest, and autumn closed into winter. The King loved to ride in the brisk, cold air and often took his daughter with him. They were returning home one day with a company of riders, hurrying because of the weather. The first snow of the year had begun to fall, softly, steadily, smoothing and spreading itself over the branches as if all the bright birds of summer were settling in drifts of white feathers.

Suddenly, in an open glade, they saw him. He was older now, a colt with a coat like silver. His head was high, his flaring nostrils sniffing the unknown snow, ears back, and eyes huge with alarm. The King reined in, holding up his hand for silence.

"Have you ever seen a colt more beautiful?" he whispered. "I must have him. Catch him!"

But already the colt had whirled and fled, as if it had dissolved into the whirling flakes themselves.

"Leave him, Your Majesty," advised Magus. "His kind must always be free."

Magus was the oldest and wisest man at court. He was said to know hidden things and words of power, and the King would usually listen to him. But not today.

"I will have him," he repeated proudly. "This forest is mine and all things in it belong to me."

In their holes and burrows and nests the wild things of the forest heard, and each laughed in its own way. As if anyone could own *them!* But Mirabelle was frightened for the silver colt.

"Sire," protested Magus, "living creatures are not to be owned. Man can keep them captive, or bribe them through their hunger, but he cannot own them. Only if they are loved they may stay with him as friends."

"You grow old, Magus," said the King, "and you talk an old man's folly. Tomorrow we shall search the whole forest."

All next day men hunted for the silver colt until, as the last light was fading, they glimpsed him drinking at a stream. Very softly, very quietly, the circle of hunters closed upon him. Skillfully, the head groom flung his coil of rope, and the noose fell neatly over the colt's head and tightened as he reared. Others ran to help him and they dragged the terrified colt up the bank. As he reached the top, he stopped kicking and stood quite still while the men drew near.

He was shivering and flecked with foam, and dark patches of sweat stained his shining flanks. Nearer came the head groom, and nearer, with gentle soothing sounds. He was almost near enough to touch him and still the colt made no move. Then, as the man reached out his hand, he gave a high, whinnying call, plunged and reared again like a fountain of silver fire. The strong rope snapped like a piece of string, he burst through the ring of his enemies with a stallion's anger and pride, and the twilight closed on the thunder of his hooves.

The King was furious when he heard what had happened. "Fools!" he stormed. "Fools, to trust only to a rope. Go again tomorrow. The snow is thicker and food in the forest must be scarce. Build a high, strong, fenced enclosure near his drinking place, hide the entrance with branches, and bait it with good, fresh hay. Hunger will bring him in."

The hunters did just as he had said. The fence was of

strong logs, nine feet high, and the entrance skillfully hidden. All day they waited until darkness came and the moon rose. Then moving softly as a deer, the silver colt slipped out between the trees and down to the stream to drink. As he climbed the bank again and blew the drops of water from his muzzle, the sweet scent of the hay floated to him. He sniffed it and waited and sniffed again. But he smelled no danger and he came closer and closer to the hidden entrance. As he reached it and began to eat, the hunters leaped out, driving him forward, and dropped the heavy entrance bar into place behind him.

"Safe at last!" said the chief huntsman. "His Majesty will be satisfied this time."

But after his first frightened plunge, the captive was trotting round and round the trap they had made, searching for an escape. Finding none, he reared, his mane and tail streaming like water in the moonlight, and he screamed with rage and fierce disdain. Again he reared and plunged; then with two great galloping strides he gathered every steel-coiled muscle and leaped as if for the stars. He was over the fence as if it was no more than a field hedge, and away and lost in the dark.

"It isn't possible!" roared the King. "No horse could leap that height. There must have been a gap in the fence."

"Sire," said Magus, "did I not tell you that this colt must run free? He is a prince among his own kind, as you are a king among yours."

"When he is broken and reined and ridden, he shall be the prince of my whole stable," retorted the King. "Use your ancient knowledge to better purpose, Magus, and tell me how I can catch him."

"Majesty, you will never do so. Only one thing will hold him—a net that will catch the wind."

"I have never heard of such a net," said the King.

But he set every weaver and spinner in the kingdom to work. They made nets of silk, of gossamer, of gold and silver thread, of thistledown woven in thousandfold thickness. But none of them could hold or catch the wind.

With each disappointment the King's desire grew, until it began to eat away his heart and make him cruel. Once again he sent for Magus.

"Old man," he said dangerously, "you have tried to cheat me. There is no such thing as a net to catch the wind. Tell me the truth this time or you shall lie in prison to the end of your days."

Magus was indeed old and frail and he feared the King's anger. He spoke slowly and unwillingly.

"Sire, I have told you the truth, though you do not understand it. But I have read in old books that there is another way."

"What other way?"

"Do not ask me, Your Majesty. Do not use it. It will end only in grief and loss."

"What other way?" insisted the King.

"It is said that the rare ones, such as he, will come willingly to a young and gentle girl who loves them, and will even rest beside her."

"Mirabelle!"

"Do not ask her. Do not make her choose between obedience to her father and her love for the silver colt."

The King smiled thinly. "She will not have to choose."

He sent at once for his daughter and talked to her with much kindness.

"The colt must run free, Mirabelle. There is no net that will catch the wind."

"I am so glad, Father. I knew you would understand at last."

The King sighed. "I meant only to honor him, to let him

be seen and admired as he should be. No one but the King himself would ever have ridden him. But now I fear he may have left the forest, for he has not been seen for many days."

"Let me look for him, Father. Perhaps he would not be afraid of me."

"Do so indeed, my child, and tell me where you find him. Take sugar and apples with you to show that you mean him no harm."

Happily Mirabelle set off. The snow had long since melted, the thrusting grass was speckled with early flowers, and the trees were full of birdsong. And there, in the glade where she had first seen him, she found the silver colt. He was grazing quietly alone in the sunlight, but lifted his head at her soft call.

She set down the bag of apples the King had given her from his own table, and held one out on the palm of her hand. His pricked ears heard the love in her voice and he answered with a soft whicker of delight. Gentle, inquiring, foot by delicate foot, he began to move toward her. He reached out his head and took the apple, while she ran her hand along the arch of his neck. She saw that his color was changing as he grew. His coat was turning to the creamy whiteness of May blossoms, and his mane and tail glimmered as pale as starlight.

"Starlight!" she whispered to him. "That's what I'll call you. Starlight!"

He nuzzled her shoulder as if he understood, and she gave him a second apple. With a sigh he folded his slender forelegs and lay down among the flowers, and Mirabelle sat beside him stroking his head. At first she thought he only wanted rest. Then she saw how still he was and how slowly he breathed, and she was gripped with sudden fear.

"Starlight! What is it? What is it? Oh, Starlight, you can't *die!*"

Her father's grooms stepped out from the trees behind her.

"Have no fear, Princess. The colt is only asleep. There was a potion in the apples that you gave him. We are here to take him to the King."

Mirabelle sprang up, crying out with grief and horror.

"No, no! You mustn't touch him. My father said he should run free."

"Free until he could be caught," said the chief groom.

All her cries and struggles were useless. They lifted the colt onto a litter and carried him back to the palace, and Mirabelle wept all the way as she followed.

As they passed through the stable courtyard the other horses threw up their heads and whinnied and trampled in their stalls as if they caught the sense of danger or excitement. But the yearling never moved, not even when they laid him down in the stable prepared for him. It was unlike the others. It was spacious and warm, but it had thick stone walls and iron doors that not even he could leap or break.

Mirabelle ran to find her father.

"Father, how could you? You have made me betray him! You have broken your own promise! He will never trust anyone again."

"Hush, child. You talk foolishly. When he is full grown no king in the world will have a horse like him. He shall be treated like a prince. He will learn to live here like the others and be happy."

"He will never be happy without his freedom," mourned Mirabelle. "Nor can I ever love you again while you hold him a prisoner."

"You will both come to your senses," said the King.

He left her and went down to the stables to rejoice in his prize. But the colt would not let him, nor any man, come near. He screamed with rage, and kicked and plunged, his dark eyes flashing angry fire, and no one dared approach him. At last, fearing the colt would hurt himself, the King sent for his daughter.

At the sound of her voice the colt became quiet, and she slipped into his stall through a narrow little door from the palace itself. It was the only entrance they dared to use until their captive was tamed. She ran to him, weeping bitterly, and clasped her arms about his neck.

"Oh, Starlight! Starlight! I didn't know! I'd never have betrayed you. Will you ever forgive me?"

The colt rubbed his beautiful head against her, while real tears ran down his velvet nose, as if he understood and shared her grief.

"They will both get over it," said the King.

But he was wrong. The colt had spent his anger, but he drooped and pined. His eyes lost their luster and his once shining coat grew dull. Mirabelle became day by day thinner and more silent, and a shadow seemed to lie over the palace.

Unable to sleep, the Princess leaned from her window one night when the moon was full. The white flowers in the garden below her glimmered as Starlight's coat had done when he was free. She could bear it no longer. She dressed and crept out through the sleeping rooms of the palace and along its dim corridors, down and down to a little door that opened into the garden. Two great dogs guarded it, but they knew her and only wagged their tails in greeting as she passed.

From the gardens it was easy to reach the stables. The iron doors of Starlight's stall had never yet been opened. It took all her strength to draw the huge bolts that held them. Her hands were torn and bleeding when at last she dragged open the doors. Moonlight flooded in, turning the straw to silver heaps and glittering in the dark eyes of the colt. He was waiting for her, poised and still, his head at last proudly lifted. His whicker of love was so low it could hardly be heard, but he breathed sweetly against her as she threw her arms round him and rubbed her face against his neck.

"Good-bye, my darling! Go now! Go quickly!"

He trotted out into the yard, quietly on his unshod hooves, like a bright reflection of the moon itself. The other horses stirred and shifted in their stalls as he passed, but made no other sound. It seemed as if they knew but would not betray him. Under the courtyard archway he stopped, and turned his head in a gesture of farewell. Then she heard the muffled drumming of his hooves as he flung into a gallop, heading for the forest like a shooting star.

There was no return for either of them now. Her father's anger would be terrible against her. With a glad but aching heart she watched the colt go. Then she drew her cloak around her and followed him, a small sad shadow fading into the dark.

The King's anger was terrible indeed when he found both the colt and his daughter gone. He sent out huntsmen to search the forest, companies of soldiers to seek and arrest the Princess, messengers to every part of the kingdom to search for news. But days drew into weeks and still nothing was heard of either of the runaways. The King's anger began to ebb into despair. Every day he himself rode in the forest, escaping from his lonely, empty palace. But he could not escape from himself. Sometimes he would sit a long time, lost in his own dark thoughts, in the glade where the colt had first been seen.

Waiting there one day, he was roused by the gentle rub of a horse's nose against his shoulder. He sprang up, full of hope. But it was only his own horse, Thunder, who had once been his favorite. Thunder could not understand or bear his master's sadness, but gave him the only comfort that he

could. And suddenly the mist of anger and disappointment cleared from the King's brain, and he looked with new eyes at his horse.

"Thunder! How could I forget you, my beauty, my pride? Yet still you are faithful to me. Forgive me, my friend."

He clapped his hand against the black column of the horse's neck, and the creature pricked up his ears and gave a little dancing step of joy to feel himself caressed as he used to be. Desire had eaten the King's heart away till it was as small as a dry nut, but in that moment it began to grow once more.

Back in the palace he sent for Magus.

"Magus, old friend, I should have listened to you long ago. My folly and desire have indeed brought grief and loss just as you warned me. I am wise too late. Tell me, is there any hope?"

"There is always hope, Your Majesty. If word reaches the Princess that she need not fear, perhaps she will return."

The King recalled all his soldiers and sent a proclamation to every town and village that the return of the Princess Mirabelle would be a day of public rejoicing. But still there was no sign of her, and the palace seemed every day more lonely and more silent.

Then the King made another proclamation, that anyone who could bring the Princess home would have half the royal treasury as a reward. Day after day sentries paced the palace walls, looking for some messenger, and heralds waited to announce his arrival. But none ever came.

It was high summer again. The King sat alone in his great hall, heartsick and weary. Suddenly a trumpet sounded, clear and shrill, from the outer walls. It was answered by another and another. A messenger at last!

Wild with hope he hurried to the palace gates, unable to wait for news. Courtiers and servants thronged there too.

Someone was riding down the road from the forest. A girl with her long hair flowing free, a girl on a white horse.

A great sigh of joy went rippling through the crowd like wind through a cornfield.

"Mirabelle!" The King would have run to meet her. But now the girl and her horse were close enough to be clearly seen, and a sudden hush fell upon all who watched. Astonishment and awe held them silent. For this was no horse of ordinary kind. His coat was as shining white as cherry blossoms in spring, his silver hooves seemed hardly to touch the ground. His mane and tail glittered like a waterfall in starlight. And from the center of his forehead sprang a single gleaming silver horn. Without saddle or bridle, he was free as the wind. He was full of pride and fire and grace, and carried the Princess in willing courtesy, not in bondage.

"The unicorn," whispered Magus. "The magical unicorn! I half knew it yet dared not hope."

"You knew it? The silver colt?"

But Mirabelle had slipped down from the unicorn's back and was running to her father.

"Father! Oh, Father, I have missed you so much. Can you forgive me?"

The King caught and held her, and all the months of sorrow fell away.

"It is I who need forgiveness," he said humbly. "My dearest child, where have you been and how have you lived all this while?"

"Starlight took care of me. He carried me away into a far country until he was full grown and we knew it was safe to return."

Her father bowed his head to the unicorn as if he too were a reigning king.

"My lord, I have done you great wrong and insult, and

you have repaid me with great good. How can I make amends?"

Magus laughed with happiness. "He will not want the promised half of your treasury, Sire."

But Mirabelle had laid her cheek against the unicorn's and listened as if he spoke to her. Then she turned to the King.

"There is one thing he desires. A great thing, if you will give it."

"If it is in my power, the gift is his."

"He wishes that all the horses in your stables may be set free to go where they will."

The King's heart nearly failed him. To lose them all, his splendid horses, his greatest pride and joy! But he had given a promise and this time he would not betray it. Sadly he gave the command.

They were led out into the sunlight, tossing their heads and dancing with delight—black and bay and chestnut and white, every one of them magnificent. And each, as he saw the unicorn, bowed his head as if to a prince.

"Free them!" commanded the King.

The grooms slipped off the bridles, and at once the whole herd streamed away over the summer grass, a foaming river of floating manes and tails and flashing hooves, exulting to be free. Some galloped straight on and were lost to sight among the forest trees. But others checked and swerved and cantered back, whickering as they came. All the King's loved favorites—Thunder and Jasmine and Blood Royal and many more—were jostling together for his caresses. Some went straight to their own grooms. The most elegant white mare of the whole herd nuzzled against the youngest stable boy, who threw his arms about her neck and kissed her in his joy at her return.

The King looked round at all of them, light of heart as he had never been before.

"They have chosen," he said. "Let each man keep the horse that loves him best."

The unicorn bent his lovely head, lowering his horn as if in salute. Then he too turned and whirled away, galloping toward the forest. They watched as he grew smaller in the distance, a moon, a star, a spark of pure white light that vanished all at once in the dense shade of the trees.

The King gave a long sigh. "Will he ever come back again?"

"He will come back," promised Mirabelle. "Whenever he wishes, he will come back."

"He will come back," echoed Magus. "For the Princess has caught him, Sire, as you have caught these horses. She has caught him with love, the net that will catch the wind."

RIDDLE

In the middle of
   the middle of
   the middle
   grows a horn!

It's a riddle of
   a riddle of
   a riddle—
   Who is born

   with a little white horse body?
   a beard just like a goat?
   a lion's tail—and hind legs
   like a graceful antelope?

   a horn that spirals upwards
   from the middle of his head
   (which begins in white and then turns black
   and finally ends up red)?

In the middle of
   the middle of
   his forehead grows a horn

And the answer
   to the riddle is
   a wondrous unicorn!

Myra Cohn Livingston

THE VALLEY OF THE UNICORNS

from *A Swiftly Tilting Planet*

by *MADELEINE L'ENGLE*

A Swiftly Tilting Planet is the third book in Madeleine L'Engle's thrilling "Time Trilogy." In this volume Charles Wallace Murray has to travel through time to prevent the outbreak of a nuclear war—a feat he accomplishes with the help of a unicorn named Gaudior.

Charles's sister, Meg, keeps track of her brother's progress through a technique called kything, which lets her experience what Charles is experiencing—a situation that can be terrifying when Charles is attacked by the horrible Echthroi.

Their main protection against the forces of evil is a rune, a kind of mystic poem, given to them by a friend of the family.

In this selection Charles Wallace, wearing a kind of coat called an anorak, first meets Gaudior and heads off on an adventure with him. During a break in their journey, in a section not included here, Charles Wallace convinces the unicorn to attempt the dangerous feat of traveling not only through time but across great distances—to a place in South America called Patagonia. Because of the increased risk of attack by Echthroi, Charles Wallace secures himself to Gaudior's back with a rope. Which is all you need to know to enjoy this selection. On with the adventure!

Charles Wallace continued to walk along the familiar route.

Hand resting on Ananda, the tingling warmth flowing back and forth between them, Meg followed her brother's steps. When he reached the open space where the star-watching rock was, Ananda's breathing quickened; Meg could feel the rise and fall of the big dog's rib cage under her hand.

There was no moon, but starlight touched the winter grasses with silver. The woods behind the rock were a dark shadow. Charles Wallace looked across the valley, across the dark ridge of pines, to the shadows of the hills beyond. Then he threw back his head and called,

"In this fateful hour
I call on all Heaven with its power!"

The brilliance of the stars increased. Charles Wallace continued to gaze upward. He focused on one star which throbbed with peculiar intensity. A beam of light as strong as a ladder but clear as water flowed between the star and Charles Wallace, and it was impossible to tell whether the light came from the piercing silver-blue of the star or the light blue eyes of the boy. The beam became stronger and firmer and then all the light resolved itself in a flash of radiance beside the boy. Slowly the radiance took on form, until it had enfleshed itself into the body of a great white beast with flowing mane and tail. From its forehead sprang a silver horn which contained the residue of the light. It was a creature of utter and absolute perfection.

The boy put his hand against the great white flanks, which heaved as though the creature had been racing. He

could feel the warm blood coursing through the veins as the light had coursed between star and boy. "Are you real?" he asked in a wondering voice.

The creature gave a silver neigh which translated itself into the boy's mind as "I am not real. And yet in a sense I am that which is the only reality."

"Why have you come?" The boy's own breath was rapid, not so much with apprehension as with excitement and anticipation.

"You called on me."

"The rune—" Charles Wallace whispered. He looked with loving appreciation at the glorious creature standing beside him on the star-watching rock. One silver-shod hoof pawed lightly, and the rock rang with clarion sound. "A unicorn. A real unicorn."

"That is what you call me. Yes."

"What are you, really?"

"What are *you*, really?" the unicorn countered. "You called me, and because there is great need, I am here."

"You know the need?"

"I have seen it in your mind."

"How is it that you speak my language?"

The unicorn neighed again, the sound translucent as silver bubbles. "I do not. I speak the ancient harmony."

"Then how is it that I understand?"

"You are very young, but you belong to the Old Music."

"Do you know my name?"

"Here, in this When and Where, you are called Charles Wallace. It is a brave name. It will do."

Charles Wallace stretched up on tiptoe to reach his arms about the beautiful beast's neck. "What am I to call you?"

"You may call me Gaudior." The words dropped on the rock like small bells.

Charles Wallace looked thoughtfully at the radiance of the horn. "Gaudior. That's Latin for *more joyful.*"

The unicorn neighed in acquiescence.

"That joy in existence without which . . ."

Gaudior struck his hoof lightly on the rock, with the sound of a silver trumpet. "Do not push your understanding too far."

"But I'm not wrong about Gaudior?"

"In a sense, yes; in a sense, no."

"You're real and you're not real; I'm wrong and I'm right."

"What is real?" Gaudior's voice was as crystal as the horn.

"What am I supposed to do, now that I've called on all Heaven with its power and you've come?"

Gaudior neighed. "Heaven may have sent me, but my powers are closely defined and narrowly limited. And I've never been sent to your planet before. It's considered a hardship assignment." He looked down in apology.

Charles Wallace studied the snow-dusted rock at his feet. "We haven't done all that well by our planet, have we?"

"There are many who would like to let you wipe yourselves out, except it would affect us all; who knows what might happen? And as long as there are even a few who belong to the Old Music, you are still our brothers and sisters."

Charles Wallace stroked Gaudior's long, aristocratic nose. "What should I do, then?"

"We're in it together." Gaudior knelt delicately and indicated that Charles Wallace was to climb up onto his back. Even with the unicorn kneeling, it was with difficulty that the boy clambered up and sat astride, up toward the great neck, so that he could hold onto the silver mane. He pressed his feet in their rubber boots as tightly as he could against the unicorn's flanks.

Gaudior asked, "Have you ridden the wind before?"

"No."

"We have to be careful of Echthroi," Gaudior warned. "They try to ride the wind and throw us off course."

"Echthroi—" Charles Wallace's eyes clouded. "That means *the enemy.*"

"Echthroi," Gaudior repeated. "The ancient enemy. He who distorted the harmony, and who has gathered an army of destroyers. They are everywhere in the universe."

Charles Wallace felt a ripple of cold move along his spine.

"Hold my mane," the unicorn advised. "There's always a possibility of encountering an Echthros, and if we do, it'll try to unseat you." Charles Wallace's knuckles whitened as he clutched the heavy mane. The unicorn began to run, skimming over the tops of the grasses, up, over the hills, flinging himself onto the wind and riding with it, up, up, over the stars . . .

The attack came almost immediately, Echthroi surrounding boy and unicorn. Charles Wallace's hands were torn from Gaudior's mane, but the rope held firm. The breath was buffeted out of him, and his eyelids were sealed tight against his eyes by the blasting wind, but the Echthroi did not succeed in pulling him off Gaudior's back. The rope strained and groaned, but the knots held.

Gaudior's breath came in silver streamers. He had folded his wings into his flanks to prevent the Echthroid wind from breaking them. Boy and unicorn were flung through endless time and space.

A cold, stenching wind picked them up and they were flung downward with a violence over which the unicorn had no control. Helplessly they descended toward a vast darkness.

They crashed.

They hit with such impact that Charles Wallace thought fleetingly, just before he lost consciousness, that the Echthroi had flung them onto rock and this was the end.

But the descent continued. Down down into blackness and cold. No breath. A feeling of strangling, a wild ringing in the ears. Then he seemed to be rising, up, up, and light. hit his closed eyes with the force of a blow, and clear cold air rushed into his lungs. He opened his eyes.

It was water and not rock they had been thrown against.

"Gaudior!" he cried, but the unicorn floated limply on the surface of the darkness, half on his side, so that one of Charles Wallace's legs was still in the water. The boy bent over the great neck. No breath came from the silver nostrils. There was no rise and fall of chest, no beat of heart. "Gaudior!" he cried in anguish. "Don't be dead! Gaudior!"

Still, the unicorn floated limply, and small waves splashed over his face.

"Gaudior!" With all his strength Charles Wallace beat against the motionless body. —The rune, he thought wildly, —the rune . . .

But no words came, except the unicorn's name. "Gaudior! Gaudior!"

A trembling stirred the silver body, and then Gaudior's breath came roaring out of him like an organ with all the stops pulled out. Charles Wallace sobbed with relief. The unicorn opened eyes which at first were glazed, then cleared and shone like diamonds. He began to tread water. "Where are we?"

Charles Wallace bent over the beautiful body, stroking neck and mane in an ecstasy of relief. "In the middle of an ocean."

"Which ocean?" Gaudior asked testily.

"I don't know."

"It's your planet. You're supposed to know."

"Is it my planet?" Charles Wallace asked. "The Echthroi had us. Are you sure we aren't in a Projection?"

Unicorn and boy looked around. The water stretched to the horizon on all sides. Above them the sky was clear, with a few small clouds.

"It's not a Projection." Gaudior whickered. "But we could be anywhere in Creation, on any planet in any galaxy which has air with oxygen and plenty of water. Does this seem to you like an ordinary earth ocean?" He shook his head, and water sprayed out from his mane. "I am not thinking clearly yet . . ." He gulped the air, then regurgitated a large quantity of salt water. "I have drunk half this ocean."

"It looks like a regular ocean," Charles Wallace said tentatively, "and it feels like winter." His drenched anorak clung to his body in wet folds. His boots were full of water, which sloshed icily against his feet. "Look!" He pointed ahead of them to a large crag of ice protruding from the water. "An iceberg."

"Which direction is land?"

"Gaudior, if we don't even know which galaxy or planet we're on, how do you expect me to know where land is?"

With difficulty Gaudior stretched his wings to their fullest extent, so that they shed water in great falls that splashed noisily against the waves. His legs churned with a mighty effort to keep afloat.

"Can you fly?" Charles Wallace asked.

"My wings are waterlogged."

"Can't you ask the wind where we are?"

A shudder rippled along the unicorn's flanks. "I'm still half winded—the wind—the wind—we hit water so hard it's a wonder all our bones aren't broken. The wind must have cushioned our fall. Are you still tied on?"

"Yes, or I wouldn't be here. Ask the wind, please."

"Winded—the wind—the wind—" Again Gaudior shook water from his wings. He opened his mouth in his characteristic gesture of drinking, gulped in the cold, clear breeze, his lips pulled back to reveal the dangerous-looking teeth. He closed his eyes and his long lashes were dark against his skin, which had paled to the color of moonlight. He opened his eyes and spat out a great fountain of water. "Thank the galaxies."

"Where are we?"

"Your own galaxy, your own solar system, your own planet. Your own Where."

"You mean this is the place of the star-watching rock? Only it's covered by an ocean?"

"Yes. And the wind says it's midsummer."

Charles Wallace looked at the iceberg. "It's a good thing it's summer, or we'd be dead from cold. And summer or no, we'll die of cold if we don't get out of water and onto land, and soon."

Gaudior sighed. "My wings are still heavy with water and my legs are tiring."

A wave dashed over them. Charles Wallace swallowed a mouthful of salty water and choked, coughing painfully. His lungs ached from the battering of the Echthroid wind and the cold of the sea. He was desperately sleepy. He thought of travelers lost in a blizzard, and how in the end all they wanted was to lie down in the snow and go to sleep, and if they gave in to sleep they would never wake up again. He struggled to keep his eyes open, but it hardly seemed worth the effort.

Gaudior's legs moved more and more slowly. When the

next wave went over them, the unicorn did not kick back up to the surface.

As water and darkness joined to blot out Charles Wallace's consciousness, he heard a ringing in his ears, and through the ringing a voice calling, "The rune, Chuck! Say it! Say the rune!"

But the weight of the icy water bore him down.

Ananda's frantic whining roused Meg.

"Say it, Charles!" she cried, sitting bolt-upright.

Ananda whined again, then gave a sharp bark.

"I'm not sure I remember the words—" Meg pressed both hands against the dog, and called out,

> *"With Ananda in this fateful hour*
> *I place all heaven with its power*
> *And the sun with its brightness,*
> *And the snow with its whiteness,*
> *And the fire with all the strength it hath,*
> *And the lightning with its rapid wrath,*
> *And the winds with their swiftness along their*
> *   path . . ."*

The wind lifted and the whitecaps were churned into rolling breakers, and unicorn and boy were raised to the surface of the water and caught in a great curling comber and swept along with it across the icy sea until they were flung onto the white sands of dry land.

Unicorn and boy vomited sea water and struggled to breathe, their lungs paining them as though they were being slashed by knives. They were sheltered from the wind by a cliff of ice onto which the sun was pouring, so that water was streaming down in little rivulets. The warmth of the sun which was melting the ice also melted the chill from their sodden bodies, and began to dry the unicorn's water-logged wings. Gradually their blood began to flow normally and they breathed without choking on salt water.

Because he was smaller and lighter (and billions of years younger, Gaudior pointed out later), Charles Wallace recovered first. He managed to wriggle out of the still-soaking anorak and drop it down onto the wet sand. Then with difficulty he kicked off the boots. He looked at the ropes which still bound him to the unicorn; the knots were pulled so tight and the cord was by now so sodden that it was impossible to untie himself. Exhausted, he bent over Gaudior's neck and felt the healing sun send its rays deep into his body. Warmed and soothed, his nose pressed against wet unicorn mane, he fell into sleep, a deep, life-renewing sleep.

When he awoke, Gaudior was stretching his wings out to the sun. A few drops of water still clung to them, but the unicorn could flex them with ease.

"Gaudior," Charles Wallace started, and yawned.

"While you were sleeping," the unicorn reproved gently, "I have been consulting the wind. Praise the Music that we're in the When of the melting of the ice or we could not have survived." He, too, yawned.

"Do unicorns sleep?" Charles Wallace asked.

"I haven't needed to sleep in aeons."

"I feel all the better for a nap. Gaudior, I'm sorry."

"For what?"

"For making you try to get us to Patagonia. If I hadn't, we might not have been nearly killed by the Echthroi."

"Apology accepted," Gaudior said briskly. "Have you learned?"

"I've learned that every time I've tried to control things we've had trouble. I don't know what we ought to do now, or Where or When we ought to go from here. I just don't know . . ."

"I think"—Gaudior turned his great head to look at the boy—"that our next step is to get all these knots untied."

Charles Wallace ran his fingers along the rope. "The knots are all sort of welded together from wind and water and sun. I can't possibly untie them."

Gaudior wriggled against the pressure of the ropes. "They appear to have shrunk. I am very uncomfortable."

After a futile attempt at what looked like the most pliable of the knots, Charles Wallace gave up. "I've got to find something to cut the rope."

Gaudior trotted slowly up and down the beach. There were shells, but none sharp enough. They saw a few pieces of rotting driftwood, and some iridescent jellyfish and clumps of seaweed. There were no broken bottles or tin cans or other signs of mankind, and while Charles Wallace was usually horrified at human waste and abuse of nature, he would gladly have found a broken beer bottle.

Gaudior turned inland around the edge of the ice cliff, moving up on slipping sand runneled by melting ice. "This is absurd. After all we've been through, who would have thought I'd end up like a centaur with you permanently affixed to my back?" But he continued to struggle up until he was standing on the great shoulder of ice.

"Look!" Charles Wallace pointed to a cluster of silvery plants with long spikes which had jagged teeth along the sides. "Do you think you could bite one of those off, so I can saw the rope with it?"

Gaudior splashed through puddles of melted ice, lowered his head, and bit off one of the spikes as close to the root as his large teeth permitted. Holding it between his teeth, he twisted his head around until Charles Wallace, straining until the rope nearly cut off his breath, managed to take it from him.

Gaudior wrinkled his lips in distaste. "It's repellent. Careful, now. Unicorn's hide is not as strong as it looks."

"Stop fidgeting."

"It itches." Gaudior flung his head about with uncontrollable and agonized laughter. "Hurry."

"If I hurry, I'll cut you. It's coming now." He moved the plant-saw back and forth with careful concentration, and finally one of the ropes parted. "I'll have to cut one more, on the other side. The worst is over now."

But when the second rope was severed, Charles Wallace was still bound to the unicorn, and the plant was limp and useless. "Can you bite off another spike?"

Gaudior bit and grimaced. "Nothing really has to taste that disagreeable. But then, I am not accustomed to any food except starlight and moonlight."

At last the ropes were off boy and beast, and Charles Wallace slid to the surface of the ice cliff. Gaudior was attacked by a fit of sneezing, and the last of the sea water flooded from his nose and mouth. Charles Wallace looked at the unicorn and drew in his breath in horror. Where the lines of rope had crossed the flanks there were red welts, shocking against the silver hide. The entire abdominal area, where the webbed hammock had rubbed was raw and oozing blood. The water which had flooded from Gaudior's nostrils was pinkish.

The unicorn in turn inspected the boy. "You're a mess," he stated flatly. "You can't possibly go Within in this condition. You'd only hurt your host."

"You're a mess, too," Charles Wallace replied. He looked at his hands, and the palms were as raw as Gaudior's belly. Where the anorak and his shirt had slipped, the rope had cut into his waist as it had cut into Gaudior's flanks.

"And you have two black eyes," the unicorn informed him. "It's a wonder you can see at all."

Charles Wallace squinted, first with one eye, then the other. "Things are a little blurry," he confessed.

Gaudior shook a few last drops from his wings. "We can't stay here, and you can't go Within now, that's obvious."

Charles Wallace looked at the sun, which was moving toward the west. "It's going to be cold when the sun goes down. And there doesn't seem to be any sign of life. And nothing to eat."

Gaudior folded his wings across his eyes and appeared to contemplate. Then he returned the wings to the bleeding flanks. "I don't understand earth time."

"What's that got to do with it?"

"Time is of the essence, we both know that. And yet it will take weeks, if not months, for us to heal."

When the unicorn stared at him as though expecting a response, Charles Wallace looked down at a puddle in the ice. "I don't have any suggestions."

"We're both exhausted. The one place I can take you without fear of Echthroi is my home. No mortal has ever been there, and I am not sure I should bring you, but it's the only way I see open to us." The unicorn flung back his mane so that it brushed against the boy's bruised face with a silver coolness. "I have become very fond of you, in spite of all your foolishness."

Charles Wallace hugged the unicorn. "I have become fond of you, too."

Joints creaking painfully, Gaudior knelt. The boy clambered up, wincing as he inevitably touched the red welts which marred the flanks. "I'm sorry. I don't want to hurt you."

Gaudior neighed softly. "I know you don't."

The boy was so exhausted that he was scarcely aware of

their flight. Stars and time swirled about him, and his lids began to droop.

"Wake up!" Gaudior ordered, and he opened his eyes to a world of starlit loveliness. The blurring of his vision had cleared, and he looked in awe at a land of snow and ice; he felt no cold, only the tenderness of a soft breeze which touched his cuts and bruises with healing gentleness. In the violet sky hung a sickle moon, and a smaller, higher moon, nearly full. Mountains heaved snow-clad shoulders skyward. Between the ribs of one of the foothills he saw what appeared to be a pile of enormous eggs.

Gaudior followed his gaze. "The hatching grounds. It has been seen by no other human eyes."

"I didn't know unicorns came from eggs," the boy said wonderingly.

"Not all of us do," Gaudior replied casually. "Only the time travelers." He took in great draughts of moonlight, then asked, "Aren't you thirsty?"

Charles Wallace's lips were cracked and sore. His mouth was parched. He looked longingly at the moonlight and tentatively opened his mouth to it. He felt a cool and healing touch on his lips, but when he tried to swallow he choked.

"I forgot," Gaudior said. "You're human. In my excitement at being home it slipped my mind." He cantered off to one of the foothills and returned with a long blue-green icicle held carefully in his teeth.

"Suck it slowly. It may sting at first, but it has healing properties."

The cool drops trickled gently down the boy's parched throat, like rays of moonlight, and at the same time that they cooled the burning, they warmed his cold body. He gave his entire concentration to the moonsicle, and when he had finished the last healing drops he turned to thank Gaudior.

The unicorn was rolling in the snow, his legs up in the air, rolling and rolling, a humming of sheer pleasure coming from his throat. Then he stood up and shook himself, flinging splashes of snow in all directions. The red welts were gone; his hide was smooth and glistening perfection. He looked at the sore places on Charles Wallace's waist and hands. "Roll, the way I did," he ordered.

Charles Wallace threw himself into the snow, which was like no other snow he had ever felt; each flake was separate and tingly; it was cool but not chilling, and he felt healing move not only over the rope burns but deep within his sore muscles. He rolled over and over, laughing with delight. Then came a moment when he knew that he was completely healed, and he jumped up. "Gaudior, where is everybody? All the other unicorns?"

"Only the time travelers come to the hatching grounds, and during the passage of the small moon they can be about other business, for the small moon casts its warmth on the eggs. I brought you here, to this place, and at this moon, so we'd be alone."

"But why should we be alone?"

"If the others saw you, they'd fear for their eggs."

Charles Wallace's head came barely halfway up the unicorn's haunches. "Creatures your size would be afraid of me?"

"Size is immaterial. There are tiny viruses which are deadly."

"Couldn't you tell them I'm not a virus and I'm not deadly?"

Gaudior blew out a gust of air. "Some of them think mankind *is* deadly."

Charles Wallace, too, sighed, and did not reply.

Gaudior nuzzled his shoulder. "Those of us who have been around the galaxies know that such thinking is foolish. It's always easy to blame others. And I have learned, being with you, that many of my preconceptions about mortals were wrong. Are you ready?"

Charles Wallace held out his hands to the unicorn. "Couldn't I see one of the eggs hatch?"

"They won't be ready until the rising of the third moon, unless . . ." Gaudior moved closer to the clutch, each egg almost as long as the boy was tall. "Wait—" The unicorn trotted to the great globular heap, which shone with inner luminosity, like giant moonstones. Gaudior bent his curved neck so that his mane brushed softly over the surface of the shells. With his upper teeth he tapped gently on one, listening, ears cocked, the short ear-hairs standing up and quivering like antennae. After a moment he moved on to another shell and then another, with unhurried patience, until he tapped on one shell twice, thrice, then drew back and nodded at the boy.

This egg appeared to have rolled slightly apart from the others, and as Charles Wallace watched, it quivered and rolled even farther away. From inside the shell came a sound of tapping, and the egg began to glow. The tapping accelerated and the shell grew so bright the boy could scarcely look at it. A sharp cracking, and a flash of brilliance as the horn thrust up and out into the pearly air, followed by a head with the silver mane clinging damply to neck and forehead. Dark silver-lashed eyes opened slowly, and the baby unicorn looked around, its eyes reflecting the light of the moons as it gazed on its fresh new environment. Then it wriggled and cracked the rest of the shell. As fragments of shell fell onto the snowy ground they broke into thousands of flakes, and the shell became one with the snow.

The baby unicorn stood on new and wobbly legs, neigh-ing a soft moonbeam sound until it gained its balance. It stood barely as tall as Charles Wallace, testing one forehoof, then the other, and kicking out its hind legs. As Charles Wallace watched, lost in delight, the baby unicorn danced under the light of the two moons.

Then it saw Gaudior, and came prancing over to the big unicorn; by slightly lowering the horn it could have run right under the full-grown beast.

Gaudior nuzzled the little one's head just below the horn. Again the baby pranced with pleasure, and Gaudior began to dance with it, leading the fledgling in steps ever more and more intricate. When the baby began to tire, Gaudior slowed the steps of the dance and raised his head to the sickle moon, drew back his lips in an exaggerated gesture and gulped moonlight.

As the baby had been following Gaudior in the steps of the dance, so it imitated him now, eagerly trying to drink moonlight, the rays dribbling from its young and inexperienced lips and breaking like crystal on the snow. Again it tried, looking at Gaudior, until it was thirstily and tidily swallowing the light as it was tipped out from the curve of the moon.

Gaudior turned to the nearly full moon, and again with exaggerated gestures taught the little one to drink. When its flanks were quivering with fullness, Gaudior turned to the nearest star, and showed it the pleasures of finishing a meal by quenching its thirst with starlight. The little one sipped contentedly, then closed its mouth with its tiny, diamond-like teeth, and, replete, leaned against Gaudior.

Only then did it notice Charles Wallace. With a leap of startlement, it landed on all four spindly legs, squealed in terror and galloped away, tail streaming silver behind it.

Charles Wallace watched the little creature disappear

over the horizon. "I'm sorry I frightened it. Will it be all right?"

Gaudior nodded reassuringly. "It's gone in the direction of the Mothers. They'll tell it you're only a bad dream it had coming out of the shell, and it'll forget all about you." He knelt.

Reluctantly Charles Wallace mounted and sat astride the great neck. Holding on to a handful of mane, he looked about at the wild and peaceful landscape. "I don't want to leave."

"You human beings tend to want good things to last forever. They don't. Not while we're in time. Do you have any instructions for me?"

"I'm through with instructions. I don't even have any suggestions."

"We'll go Where and When the wind decides to take us, then?"

"What about Echthroi?" Charles Wallace asked fearfully.

"Because we're journeying from the home place the wind should be unmolested, as it was when we came here. After that we'll see. We've been in a very deep sea, and I never thought we'd get out of it. Try not to be afraid. The wind will give us all the help it can." The wings stretched to their full span and Gaudior flew up between the two moons, and away from the unicorn hatching grounds.

RAGGED JOHN

Tattered clothes all fluttering
Worn out voice still muttering
Ragged John comes knocking
At all the doors in town.

And when a door swings open
Then you can hear the hope in
The thin, cracked voice that wonders
If you've seen his unicorn.

And we all know John is crazy
And his mind has gone all hazy
And the only thing we really wish
Is that he just would let us be.

But John, he keeps on questing
And the poor man knows no resting
For there's something hurt within him.
And the pain won't go away.

I've heard when John was younger
He was taken with a hunger
To see the white-horned wonder
They call the unicorn.

But when that star-horned, moon-maned dancer
Finally called, John could not answer;
Fear held him like a prisoner,
And he watched it walk away.

So now empty-eyed John hobbles
Across the village cobbles,
And the only fear he feels is
It will never come again.

Oh, when I watch old Ragged John
Go staggering by and wandering on,
I know there's nothing sadder
Than a heart that feared its dreams.

If a unicorn should call to you
Some moon-mad night all washed in dew,
Then here's the prayer to whisper:
Grant me the heart to follow.

Beatrice Farrington

HOMEWARD BOUND

by BRUCE COVILLE

Jamie stood on the steps of his uncle's house and looked up. The place was tall and bleak. With its windows closed and shuttered, as they were now, it was easy to imagine the building was actually trying to keep him out.

"This isn't home," he thought rebelliously. "It's not home, and it never will be."

A pigeon fluttered onto the lawn nearby. Jamie started, then frowned. His father had raised homing pigeons, and the two of them had spent many happy hours together, tending his flock. The sight of the bird now, with the loss of his father still so fresh in his mind, only stirred up memories he wasn't ready to deal with yet.

He looked at the house again and was struck by an odd feeling: while this wasn't home, coming here had somehow taken him one step closer to finding it. That feeling had to do with the horn, of course; of that much he was certain.

Jamie was seven the first time he had seen the horn hanging on the wall of his uncle's study.

"Narwhal," said his uncle, following the boy's gaze. "It's a whale with a horn growing out of the front of its head." He put one hand to his forehead and thrust out a finger to illustrate, as if Jamie were some sort of an idiot. "Sort of a seagoing unicorn," he continued. "Except, of course, that it's real instead of imaginary. I'd rather you didn't touch it. I paid dearly to get it."

Jamie had stepped back behind his father without speaking. He hadn't dared to say what was on his mind. Grown-ups, especially his uncle, didn't like to be told they were wrong.

But his uncle *was* wrong. The horn had not come from a narwhal, not come from the sea at all.

It was the horn of a genuine unicorn.

Jamie couldn't have explained how he knew this was so. But he did, as surely—and mysteriously—as his father's pigeons knew their way home. Thinking of that moment of certainty now, he was reminded of those stormy nights when he and his father had watched lightning crackle through the summer sky. For an instant, everything would be outlined in light. Then, just as quickly, the world would be plunged back into darkness, with nothing remaining but a dazzling memory.

That was how it had been with the horn, five years ago.

And now Jamie was twelve, and his father was dead, and he had been sent to live with this rich, remote man who had always frightened him so much.

Oddly, that fear didn't come from his uncle. Despite his stern manner, the man was always quiet and polite with Jamie. Rather he had learned it from his father. The men had not been together often, for his uncle frequently disappeared on mysterious "business trips" lasting weeks or even months on end. But as he watched his father grow nervous and unhappy whenever his brother returned, Jamie came to sense that the one man had some strange hold over the other.

It frightened him.

Yet as scared as he was, as sad and lonely over the death of his father, one small corner of his soul was burning now with a fierce joy, because he was finally going to be close to the horn.

Of course, in a way, he had never been apart from it. Ever

since that first sight, five years ago, the horn had shimmered
in his memory. It was the first thing he thought of when he
woke up, and the last at night when he went to sleep. It was
a gleaming beacon in his dreams, reassuring him no matter
how cruel and ugly a day might have been, there was a
reason to go on, a reason to be. His one glimpse of the horn
had filled him with a sense of beauty and rightness so powerful it had carried him through these five years.

Even now, while his uncle was droning on about the
household rules, he saw it again in that space in the back of
his head where it seemed to reside. Like a shaft of never-
ending light, it tapered through the darkness of his mind,
wrist thick at its base, ice-pick sharp at its tip, a spiraled
wonder of icy, pearly whiteness. And while Jamie's uncle
was telling him the study was off-limits, Jamie was trying to
figure out how quickly he could slip in there to see the horn
again.

For once again his uncle was wrong. No place that held
the horn could be off-limits for him. It was too deeply a part
of him.

That was why he had come here so willingly, despite his
fear of his uncle. Like the pigeons, he was making his way
home.

Jamie listened to the big clock downstairs as it marked off
the quarter hours. When the house had been quiet for sev-
enty-five minutes he took the flashlight from under his pillow, climbed out of bed and slipped on his robe. Walking
softly, he made his way down the hall, enjoying the feel of
the thick carpet like moss beneath his feet.

He paused at the door of the study. Despite his feelings,

he hesitated. What would his uncle say, or do, if he woke and caught him here?

The truth was, it didn't matter. He had no choice. He had to see the horn again.

Turning the knob of the door, he held his breath against the inevitable click. But when it came, it was mercifully soft. He stepped inside, and flicked on his flashlight.

His heart lurched as the beam struck the opposite wall and showed an empty place where the horn had once hung. A little cry slipped through his lips before he remembered how important it was to remain silent.

He swung the light around the room, and breathed a sigh of relief. The horn, the alicorn, as his reading had told him it was called, lay across his uncle's desk.

He stepped forward, almost unable to believe that the moment he had dreamed of all these years was finally at hand.

He took another step, and another.

He was beside the desk now, close enough to reach out and touch the horn.

And still he hesitated.

Part of that hesitation came from wonder, for the horn was even more beautiful than he had remembered. Another part of it came from a desire to make this moment last as long as he possibly could. It was something he had been living toward for five years now, and he wanted to savor it. But the biggest part of his hesitation came from fear. He had a sense that once he had touched the horn, his life might never be the same again.

That didn't mean he wouldn't do it.

But he needed to prepare himself. So for a while he simply stood in the darkness, gazing at the horn. Light seemed to play beneath its surface, as if there was something alive inside it—though how that could be after all this time he didn't know.

Finally he reached out to stroke the horn. Just stroke it. He wasn't ready, yet, to truly embrace whatever mystery was waiting for him. Just a hint, just a teasing glimpse, was all he wanted.

His fingertip grazed the horn and he cried out in terror as the room lights blazed on, and his uncle's powerful voice thundered over him, demanding to know what was going on.

Jamie collapsed beside the desk. His uncle scooped him up and carried him back to his room.

A fever set in, and it was three days before Jamie got out of bed again.

He had vague memories of people coming to see him during that time—of a doctor who took his pulse and temperature; of an older woman who hovered beside him, spooning a thin broth between his lips and wiping his forehead with a cool cloth; and most of all, of his uncle, who loomed over his bed like a thundercloud, glowering down at him.

His only other memories were of the strange dream that gripped him over and over again, causing him to thrash and cry out in terror. In the dream he was running through a deep forest. Something was behind him, pursuing him. He leaped over mossy logs, splashed through cold streams, crashed through brambles and thickets. But no matter how he tried, he couldn't escape the fierce thing that was after him—a thing that wore his uncle's face.

More than once Jamie sat up in bed, gasping and covered with sweat. Then the old woman, or the doctor, would speak soothing words and try to calm his fears.

Once he woke quietly. He could hear doves cooing outside his window. Looking up, he saw his uncle standing beside the bed, staring down at him angrily.

"Why?" wondered Jamie. "Why doesn't he want me to touch the horn?"

But he was tired, and the question faded as he slipped back into his dreams.

He was sent away to a school, where he was vaguely miserable but functioned well enough to keep the faculty at a comfortable distance. The other students, not so easily escaped, took some delight in trying to torment the dreamy boy who was so oblivious to their little world of studies and games, their private wars and rages. After a while they gave it up; Jamie didn't react enough to make their tortures worth the effort on any but the most boring of days.

He had other things to think about, memories and mysteries that absorbed him and carried him through the year, aware of the world around him only enough to move from one place to another, to answer questions, to keep people away.

The memories had two sources. The first was the vision that had momentarily dazzled him when he touched the horn, a tantalizing instant of joy so deep and powerful it had shaken him to the roots of his being. Hints of green, of cool, of wind in face and hair whispered at the edges of that vision.

He longed to experience it again.

The other memories echoed from his fever dreams, and were not so pleasant. They spoke only of fear, and some terrible loss he did not understand.

Christmas, when it finally came, was difficult. As the other boys were leaving for home, his uncle sent word that urgent business would keep him out of town throughout the holiday. He paid the headmaster handsomely to keep an eye on Jamie, and feed him Christmas dinner.

The boy spent a bleak holiday longing for his father. Until now his obsession with the horn had shielded him from the still raw pain of that loss. But the sounds and smells of the holiday, the tinkling bells, the warm spices, the temporary but real good will surrounding him, all stirred the sorrow inside him, and he wept himself to sleep at night.

He would dream. In his dreams his father would reach out to take his hand. "We're all lost," he would whisper, as he had the day he died. "Lost, and aching to find our name, so that we can finally go home again."

When Jamie woke, his pillow would be soaked with sweat, and tears.

The sorrow faded with the return of the other students, and the resumption of a daily routine. Even so, it was a relief when three months later his uncle sent word that he would be allowed to come back for the spring holiday.

The man made a point of letting Jamie know he had hidden the horn by taking him into the study soon after his arrival at the house. He watched closely as the boy's eyes flickered over the walls, searching for the horn, and seemed satisfied at the expression of defeat that twisted his face before he closed in on himself, shutting out the world again.

But Jamie had become cunning. The defeat he showed his uncle was real. What the man didn't see, because the boy buried it as soon as he was aware of it, was that the defeat was temporary. For hiding the horn didn't make any difference. Now that Jamie had touched it, he was bound to it. Wherever it was hidden, he would find it. Its call was too powerful to mistake.

Even so, Jamie thought he might lose his mind before he got his chance. Day after day his uncle stayed in the house, guarding his treasure. Finally, on the morning of the fifth day, an urgent message pulled him away. Even then, the anger that burned in his face as he stormed through the great oak doors, an anger Jamie knew was rooted in being called from his vigil, might have frightened someone less determined.

The boy didn't care. He would make his way to the horn while he had the chance.

He knew where it was, of course—had known from the evening of the first day.

It was in his uncle's bedroom.

The room was locked. Moving cautiously, Jamie slipped downstairs to the servant's quarters and stole the master key, then scurried back to the door. To his surprise he felt no fear.

He decided it was because he had no choice; he was only doing what he had to do.

He twisted the key in the lock and swung the door open.

His uncle's room was large and richly decorated, filled with heavy, carefully carved furniture. Above the dresser hung a huge mirror.

Jamie hesitated for just a moment, then lay on his stomach and peered beneath the bed.

The horn was there, wrapped in a length of blue velvet.

He reached in and drew the package out. Then he stood, and placed it gently on the bed. With reverent fingers he unrolled the velvet. Cradled by the rich blue fabric, the horn looked like a comet blazing across a midnight sky.

This time there could be no interruption. Hesitating for no more than a heartbeat, he reached out and clutched the horn with both hands.

He cried out, in agony, and in awe. For a moment he thought he was going to die. The feelings the horn unleashed within him seemed too much for his body to hold. He didn't die, though his heart was racing faster than it had any right to.

"More," he thought, as images of the place he had seen in his dreams rushed through his mind. "I have to know more."

He drew the horn to his chest, and laid his cheek against it.

He thought his heart would beat its way out of his body. And still it wasn't enough.

He knew what he had to do next. But he was afraid.

Fear made no difference. He remembered again what his father had said about people aching to find their true name. He was close to his now. "No one can come this close and not reach out for the answer," he thought. "The emptiness would kill them on the spot."

And so he did what he had to do, fearful as it was. Placing the base of the horn against the foot of the massive bed, he set the tip of it against his heart.

Then he leaned forward.

The point of the horn pierced his flesh like a sword made of fire and ice. He cried out, first in pain, then in joy and wonder. Finally the answer was clear to him, and he understood his obsession, and his loneliness.

"No wonder I didn't fit," he thought, as his fingers fused, then split into cloven hooves.

The transformation was painful. But the joy so far surpassed it that he barely noticed the fire he felt as his neck began to stretch, and the horn erupted from his brow. "No wonder, no wonder, no, it's all wonder, wonder, wonder and joy!"

He reared back in triumph, his silken mane streaming

behind him, as he trumpeted the joyful discovery that he was, and always had been, and always would be, a unicorn.

And knowing his name, he finally knew how to go home. Hunching the powerful muscles of his hind legs, he launched himself toward the dresser. His horn struck the mirror, and it shattered into a million pieces that crashed and tinkled into two different worlds.

He hardly noticed. He was through, and home at last.

"No," said a voice at the back of his head. "You're not home yet."

He stopped. It was true. He wasn't home yet, though he was much closer. But there was still more to do, and further to go.

How could that be? He knew he was, had always been, a unicorn. Then he trembled, as he realized his father's last words were still true. There was something inside that needed to be discovered, to be named.

He whickered nervously as he realized all he had really done was come back to where most people begin—his own place, his own shape.

He looked around. He was standing at the edge of a clearing in an old oak wood. Sunlight filtered through the leaves, dappling patches of warmth onto his flanks. He paused for a moment, taking pleasure in feeling his own true shape at last.

Suddenly he shivered, then stood stock-still as the smell of the girl reached his nostrils.

The scent was sweet, and rich, and he could resist it no more than he had resisted the horn. He began trotting in her direction, sunlight bouncing off the horn that jutted out from his forehead.

He found her sitting beneath an apple tree, singing to herself while she brushed her honey-colored hair. Doves rustled and cooed at the edges of the clearing. They reminded him of the pigeons his father had raised.

As he stood and watched her, every fiber of his being cried out that there was danger here. But it was not in the nature of a unicorn to resist such a girl.

Lowering his head, he walked forward.

"So," she said. "You've come at last."

He knelt beside her, and she began to stroke his mane. Her fingers felt cool against his neck, and she sang to him in a voice that seemed to wash away old sorrows. He relaxed into a sweet silence, content for the first time that he could remember.

He wanted the moment to go on forever.

But it ended almost instantly as the girl slipped a golden bridle over his head, and his uncle suddenly stepped into the clearing.

The man was wearing a wizard's garb, which didn't surprise Jamie. Ten armed soldiers stood behind him.

Jamie sprang to his feet. But he had been bound by the magic of the bridle; he could neither run, nor attack.

Flanks heaving, he stared at his wizard uncle.

"Did you really think you could get away from me?" asked the man.

"I have!" thought Jamie fiercely, knowing the thought would be understood.

"Don't be absurd!" snarled his uncle. "I'll take your horn, as I did your father's. And then I'll take your shape, and finally your memory. You'll come back with me, and be no different than he was—a dreamy, foolish mortal, lost and out of place."

"Why?" thought Jamie. "Why would anyone want to hold a unicorn?"

His uncle didn't answer.

Jamie locked eyes with him, begging him to explain.

No answer came. But he realized he had found a way to survive. Just as the golden bridle held him helpless, so his gaze could hold his uncle. As long as he could stare into the man's eyes, he could keep him from moving.

He knew, too, that as soon as he flinched, the battle would be over.

Jamie had no idea how long the struggle actually lasted. They seemed to be in a place apart, far away from the clearing, away from the girl, and the soldiers.

He began to grow fearful. Sooner or later he would falter and his uncle would regain control. It wasn't enough to hold him. He had to conquer him.

But how? How?

He couldn't win unless he knew why he was fighting. He had to discover why his uncle wanted to capture and hold him.

But the only way to do that was to look deeper inside the man. The idea frightened him; he didn't know what he would find there. Even worse, it would work two ways. He couldn't look deeper into his uncle, without letting his uncle look more deeply into him.

He hesitated. But there was no other way. Accepting the risk, he opened himself to his uncle.

At the same time, he plunged into the man's soul.

His uncle cried out, then dropped to his knees and buried his face in his hands, trembling with the humiliation of being seen.

Jamie trembled too, for the emptiness he found inside this man could swallow suns and devour planets. This was the hunger that had driven him to capture unicorns, in the hope that their glory could fill his darkness.

Then, at last, Jamie knew what he must do. Stepping forward, he pressed the tip of his horn against his uncle's heart.

He had been aware of his horn's healing power, of course. But this was the first time he had tried to use it. He wasn't expecting the shock of pain that jolted through him, or the wave of despair that followed as he took in the emptiness, and the fear and the hunger that had driven his uncle for so long.

He wanted to pull away, to run in terror.

But if he did, it would only start all over again. Only a healing would put an end to the pursuit. And this was the only way to heal this man, this wizard, who, he now understood, had never really been his uncle, but only his captor. He had to be seen, in all his sorrow and his ugliness; seen, and accepted, and loved. Only then could he be free of the emptiness that made him want to possess a unicorn.

Jamie trembled as the waves of emptiness and sorrow continued to wash through him. But at last he was nearly done. Still swaying from the effort, he whispered to the man: "Go back. Go back and find your name. And then—go *home.*"

That was when the sword fell, slicing through his neck.

It didn't matter, really, though he felt sorry for his "uncle," who began to weep, and sorrier still for the soldier who had done the deed. He knew it would be a decade or so before the man could sleep without mind-twisting nightmares of the day he had killed a unicorn.

But for Jamie himself, the change made no difference. Because he still was what he had always been, what he always would be, what a unicorn had simply been an appropriate shape to hold. He was a being of power and light.

He shook with delight as he realized that he had named himself at last.

He turned to the wizard, and was amazed. No longer hampered by mere eyes, he could see that the same thing was true for him—as it was for the girl, as it was for the soldiers.

They were *all* beings of power and light.

The terrible thing was, they didn't know it.

Suddenly he understood. This was the secret, the unnamed thing his father had been trying to remember: that we are all beings of power and light. And all the pain, all the sorrow—it all came from not knowing this simple truth.

Why? wondered Jamie. *Why don't any of us know how beautiful we really are?*

And then even that question became unimportant, because his father had come to take him home, and suddenly he wasn't just a unicorn, but was all unicorns, was part of every wise and daring being that had worn that shape and that name, every unicorn that had ever lived, or ever would live. And he felt himself stretch to fill the sky, as the stars came tumbling into his body, stars at his knees and at his hooves, at his shoulder and his tail, and most of all a shimmer of stars that lined the length of his horn, a horn that stretched across the sky, pointing out, for anyone who cared to look, the way to go home.

THE PAINT BOX

"Cobalt and umber and ultramarine,
Ivory black and emerald green—
What shall I paint to give pleasure to you?"
"Paint for me somebody utterly new."

"I have painted you tigers in crimson and white."
"The colors were good and you painted aright."
"I have painted the cook and a camel in blue
And a panther in purple." "You painted them true.

Now mix me a color that nobody knows,
And paint me a country where nobody goes.
And put in it people a little like you,
Watching a unicorn drinking the dew."

E. V. Rieu

THE TRANSFIGURED HART

(excerpt)

by *JANE YOLEN*

Richard Plante is a loner. Heather Fielding is a lively, popular girl from a large family.

The two of them are brought together by their discovery of a white hart that frequents a pool in the nearby woods—a hart both youngsters believe is really a unicorn.

Richard and Heather's fragile friendship is endangered when she lets their secret slip to her brothers, who are avid hunters. To the horror of both children, the older boys make plans to bag the hart on the first day of hunting season.

What happens when Richard and Heather, acting independently of one another, try to protect the unicorn forms the core of Jane Yolen's award-winning story.

Richard felt a pain in his chest, but he did not stop and he barely noticed the dark. He knew he could not possibly run all the way home, but to keep warm, he jogged slowly, willing the pain to go away. The rhythm, the pace, finally eased the ache, and it went, a little at a time. He was left with a feeling of exhilaration that surprised him. He guessed it was a combination of the crisp night air, the full moon, and the thought of what was to come. What had to come. People lay behind him; only the unicorn lay ahead. He would have to take action, something he had never really done before. It was like a quest, an adventure, a heroic journey. He could count on no one else in this, certainly not on Heather, who had betrayed them at their first real trial. He could count only on himself.

It pleased him that this time, he, Richard Plante, would be doing this. Not reading about someone else in a book, hiding his fears in silent retreat from the world and its questions. He had the answer and he was giving it loud and clear.

As he thought, planned, what he had to do in the dark night ahead, a car flashed past him, the light suddenly blinding. Then the car turned and cruised up beside him.

Of course it was Uncle Hugh, phoned by the Fieldings. Richard slipped gratefully into the car's warmth. This was no compromise. He could do nothing until near midnight, when everyone was asleep.

Uncle Hugh did not speak, not when Richard got into the car and not later, when Aunt Marcie enfolded him in a hug calculated to drive out his demons.

For once, Aunt Marcie was silent, too, except for her eyebrows, which worked up and down overtime. But Richard did not start any conversation, though he knew they were waiting for him to do so. Wordlessly, he went upstairs to bed.

He heard Uncle Hugh say, as he went up the dark stairs alone and totally unafraid, "He didn't say a thing. You'd think he'd have some explanation. I guess we'll wait till tomorrow and then we'll try and get his side of it." Richard could only guess at Aunt Marcie's eyebrows as she snorted in return "Young love!" and dialed the phone.

But none of it touched Richard as he marched up the stairs slowly and deliberately. He paused at the top landing and saluted the ghosts of his mother and father, whom he knew must hover somewhere in the house. Then he went into his room, closed the door firmly, and went to bed.

But not to sleep. No, not to sleep. For many long minutes, Richard waited for his aunt and uncle to go to bed. They would turn in early tonight. Uncle Hugh had never missed an opening of deer season yet, or so was his boast. The creak of the stairs, the shuffling in and out of the bathroom, the slight sighings and whisperings, the click of the closing door, were the signals Richard waited for. And after the noises ceased, he waited some more—twenty times sixty heartbeats—before he got out of bed.

He got up cautiously in case anyone was still awake. But his every move was ritual. He dressed in his good blue trousers and his blue jacket with the crest on it that Uncle Hugh had brought back from England. He put on his heaviest socks and boots. And for warmth, since he had left his coat at the Fieldings' house, he tossed his navy blue blanket around his shoulders like a cape. It hung in graceful folds to his ankles. Then he tiptoed down the stairs and out into the night.

The night was cold and crisp but windless. Richard walked briskly toward the path where he would turn off into the orchard. No cars passed by him as he walked, nor could he hear any of the usual night noises. There was just darkness and silence, heavy, palpable and real.

In the daytime, coming down the path, he had often stumbled. But he did not stumble now. He walked with authority. And even the brambles, dried and stiff, did not catch his makeshift cape. He did not make a single wrong twist or turn or misstep, and he came at last to the shimmering pool watched only by the moon which hung like a blind eye in the blue-black socket of sky.

Heather leaned her back against the oak door. She looked straight ahead but could see nothing through her tears. No one in the family spoke to her, or if they did, she couldn't hear them. Snuffling faintly, she went up to her room.

She lay down on the bed and stared at the bright yellow canopy. When she had been much younger, she had played at being a Princess in her room. But now it was as if the sky had fallen and was waiting, old and yellow, to crush her utterly. She turned over on her stomach and put her hands under her head.

It was then that she discovered she was still clutching the wine-stained dinner napkin. She raised up on her elbows and looked at it thoughtfully. She was still thoughtful when she took off her clothes and climbed into her nightgown. It was long and white, with a shirring of lace and a yellow ribbon woven about the neck and a yellow tie at the waist.

Slowly she unplaited her braids. Her hair, so long bound, fell over her shoulders in dark shining waves and reached down to the small of her back.

Heather sat down again on the bed and smoothed the damask napkin on her lap. The red stain in the soft light of her room looked black, but it still had the sickly sweet smell of wine.

Heather shook her head vigorously, as if to shake off her imagings, and turned off the light. Then she lay down on the bed, tucked the napkin in her bodice and remained unmoving in the dark.

A knock sounded on her door. Her mother came in. "Heather, dear, do you want to talk? Is there anything I can do?"

Heather willed her voice to calmness, firmness. "No,

Mother. I'm all right. Really I am. We'll talk tomorrow. Please."

Mrs. Fielding knew her daughter well enough to leave then. Heather could hear whisperings in the hall. Her father and then the boys cursed Richard for a coward and a fool and asked about her. She knew her mother would make them leave her alone. At least until morning. Even so, that would barely be enough time for what had to be done.

For Heather knew that she and she alone had to act. And she had to act that night if she was to save the unicorn from the hunters—from her brothers and her father and all the rest. She could not count on Richard; he *was* a coward and a fool, just as her brothers had said. A coward not to back her up, a fool to think she had let the secret slip on purpose. That she had, indeed, let the secret out was a pain she would have to bear alone. As penance, she would have to save the unicorn alone, too. So she waited out the ticking of her bedroom clock and kept herself awake.

The clock was barely touching eleven when the silence in the house told her everyone else was asleep. The boys and her father, she knew, always went to bed early the night before Opening Day. They had to rise before dawn. And her mother would be rising with them to fix them breakfast. It was a tradition never broken.

Heather got up and slipped her feet into boots. She moved silently downstairs, grabbed her heavy school cape from the closet, and was gone before the dog had time for more than a sleepy, growling yawn.

She did not take Hop out of the barn. He would hate to be disturbed for a night ride. And the heavy clopping of his hooves might alert someone in the house. Though she had to be back before one of the early risers noticed she was gone, silence was no less important than speed.

She ran down the road, her dark cape floating behind her

like bat's wings, the white gown luminous in the dark. She was lucky that no cars passed as she ran. And when, out of breath and trembling slightly from the cold, she came to the path through the apple orchard, the moon came out from behind a cloud. It was full and bright, and in the shadows it cast, the linen dinner napkin tucked in her bodice glistened both white and black.

Heather was careful not to make a misstep as she went down the path toward the pool. She stepped on nothing that might crackle or snap. And when she came at last to the clearing where the pool was set like a jewel in a ring, Richard was there before her.

"You!" they said together. But in the single word was both surprise and forgiveness.

Richard hesitated, then took the blanket off his shoulders and spread it on the ground under the wild apple tree. They both sat down, hands folded, silent and waiting.

And then it came.

White and gleaming, stepping through fragrant sweet violets, the unicorn came.

It was high at the shoulder, with a neck both strong and thick. Its face was that of a goat or a deer, like neither and yet like both, with a tassel of white hair for a beard and eyes the color of old gold. Its slim legs ended in cloven hooves that shone silver in the moonlight. Its tail was long and fringed at the tip with hair as soft and fine as silken thread. And where it stepped, flowers sprang up, daisies and lilies and the wild strawberry, and plants that neither Richard nor Heather had seen before but knew at once, the cuckoo-point and columbine and the wild forest rose.

But it was the horn that caught their gaze. The spiraled,

ivory horn that thrust from the unicorn's head, that looked both cruel and kind. It was the horn that convinced them both that this could be no dream.

And so it came, the unicorn, more silent than night yet sweeter than singing. It came 'round the shimmering pool and knelt in front of the children as they sat breathless on the blanket. It knelt before them not in humility but in fealty, and placed its head gently, oh so gently, in Heather's lap.

At the unicorn's touch, Heather sighed. And at her sigh, the silent woods around suddenly seemed to burst with the song of birds—thrush, and sparrow, and the rising meadowlark. And from far off, the children heard the unfamiliar jug-jug-jug of a nightingale.

And it was spring and summer in one. Richard looked around and saw that within the enclosure of the green meadow, ringed about with a stone wall, encircled in stone arms, was a season he had never seen before. The glade was dappled with thousands of flowers. He could see, from where he sat, pomegranate and cherry trees, orange and apple, all in full bloom. The smell of them in the air was so strong that he was almost giddy.

But Heather seemed to notice none of this. She had taken the yellow ribbon from her waist and bound it about the unicorn's head like a golden halter, over the forehead and around the soft white muzzle. Her fingers moved slowly but surely as she concentrated on the white head that lay on her lap, the horn carefully tucked under her arm. She stroked the unicorn's gleaming neck with her free hand and crooned over and over, "You beauty, you love, you beauty." And the beast closed its eyes and shuddered once and then lay very still. She could feel the veins in its silken neck under her hand, pulsing, surging, but the great white head did not move.

Richard looked over at the beast and the girl, and on his knees he moved across the blanket to them. Hesitantly, he reached his hand out toward the unicorn's neck. And Heather looked up then and took his hand in hers and placed it on the soft, smooth neck. Richard smiled shyly, then broadly, and Heather smiled back.

As they sat there, the three, without a word, a sudden harsh note halloed from afar.

"A horn," Richard said, drawing his hand away quickly. "Heather, I heard a hunting horn."

But she seemed not to hear.

The horn sounded again, nearer. There was no mistaking its insistent cry.

"Heather!"

"Oh, Richard, I hear it. What shall we do?"

The unicorn opened its eyes, eyes of antique gold. It looked steadily up at Heather, but still it did not move.

Heather tried to push the heavy head off her lap. "You have to go. You *have* to. It must be near day. The hunters will kill you. They won't care that you're beautiful. They'll just want your horn. Oh, please. *Please.*" The last was an anguished cry, but still the unicorn did not move. It was as though it lay under a spell that was too old, too powerful to break.

"Richard, it won't move. What can we do? It'll be killed. It'll be our fault. Oh, Richard, what have you read about this? Think. *Think.*"

Richard thought. He went over lists and lists in his mind. But he did not recall it in any of his reading. And then he remembered the unicorn tapestries Heather had found in her mother's art books. She had brought the book for them both to see. The unicorn had indeed been killed, slaughtered by men with sharp spears and menacing faces. What could he and Heather do about such evil?

Heather was leaning over the unicorn's neck and crying. "Oh, my beauty. Oh, forgive me. I didn't mean you to be killed. Before I saw you, really saw you, I wanted to tame you. But now I . . . we want to save you."

Richard watched her stroke the neck, the head, her hand moving hypnotically over the gleaming white, tangling in the yellow ribbon.

Suddenly Richard knew. "Heather," he shouted, "the yellow ribbon! It's the golden bridle. Take it off. Take it off!"

Heather looked at the ribbon and in that moment understood. She ripped it from the unicorn's neck. "Go!" she said. "Be free." The ribbon caught on the spiraled horn.

The minute the ribbon was off its neck, the unicorn got up heavily from its knees. It flung its head abruptly backward and the golden band flew through the air.

The ribbon landed in the middle of the pool and was sucked downward into the water with a horrible sound. The birds rose up mourning from the trees as, in a clatter of hooves, the unicorn circled the pool once, leaped over the stone wall, and disappeared.

In an instant it was November again, brown, sere, and cold.

And the pool was no longer crystal and shimmering but a dank, brackish bog the color of rotted logs.

The horn sounded again, only this time it was clearly a car horn. Loud, insistent, it split the air over and over as the sun rose, shaded in fog, over the far mountains.

"It's day," said Richard heavily. "Opening Day."

"But it's all right," said Heather, soothingly. "The unicorn is gone. It's gone forever."

"How do you know?"

"I know because I believe. Even without much practice, I believe." Heather put out her hand to Richard and he took it. Then they curled together for warmth and fell asleep in the dawn.

THE UNICORN

While yet the Morning Star
Flamed in the sky
A unicorn went mincing by,
Whiter by far than blossom of the thorn:
His silver horn
Glittered as he danced and pranced
Silver-pale in the silver-pale morn.

The folk that saw him, ran away.
Where he went, so gay, so fleet,
Star-like lilies at his feet
Flowered all day,
Lilies, lilies in a throng,
And the wind made for him a song:

But he dared not stay
Over-long!

Ella Young

THE SNOW WHITE PONY

by ARDATH MAYHAR

I had my head in the lap of a very beautiful young woman, who was braiding flowers into my mane, when the summons came. It should have irritated me more than it did, for I am extremely partial to that particular pastime.

Summonses from the Top are not that frequent, however. Few are called, and even fewer are chosen for specific tasks among troubled human beings. I, being one of the youngest of the unicorn kind, had never been called before. I went at a brisk trot through the Forest Subliminal to the glade where the oldest of my kind makes his home.

He was grazing thoughtfully on a bank of dandelions and daisies when I approached, and he finished his mouthful and shook free the fragments before taking the time to survey me.

"One of the young ones," he said, his tone disapproving. "But you were recommended for the job. I suppose I must agree. Come here."

I went forward cautiously. His temper, after so many thousands of years of life, was tricky. More than once, I had received a sharp rap from his horn . . . sometimes in spots that tingled for days afterward.

"What task am I to do?" I asked. I was a bit nervous. If we of the unicorn sort are called in, the case is usually one that the humans have given up as hopeless. It would, I felt, be very helpful to know what it was I must try to do.

"It is usually best to read the situation for yourself," he said. "However, in this one I will give you a clue. The child is no longer physically ill, yet she is dying, nevertheless. She has given up her will to live." He poked me in the side with the tip of his shiny horn and prodded me into position.

"Disguise . . . white pony. Best for this case, we think," he said. "Now shut up and be still."

I felt giddy. I had been called from my quiet life, my pleasant pastimes to be put under a spell and sent who-knew-where to do a task I had no idea how to perform . . . and without even time to polish my horn or pare my hooves. I felt as I suspect a person might feel if sent away without time to pack clean underwear or a toothbrush.

The glade became very still. Even the bees above the daisies stopped humming. A shiver went over me from horn to fetlocks. Then the glade was busy with hums and chirps and the whispers of breezes. My elder stepped away, looking tired.

"There," he said. "You're ready. Be careful not to poke anyone with your horn . . . it's invisible, but it's still there. Now go up through the glade and into the Temporal World. I've arranged for you to emerge in just the right spot."

There was nothing left to do but go. When I came through the fringe of birch and alder beyond the glade, I found myself standing on bare soil, trodden hard by many hooves before mine. There was an ugly fence of metal links. Beyond it was a paved street leading into a stand of trees that looked dusty and shopworn. A park? I suspected as much. Around me were many ponies, all tired-looking, and out on the dirt track I could see in the park even more moved slowly, carrying human children on their backs.

I felt that someone was watching me from behind. Pretending to be looking for the watering trough, I turned to amble through the other ponies. Brown, black, gray . . . I was the only white one there. Beyond another fence stood three human beings . . . real ones, not figments of the imagination.

They were staring at me. A thin white pony was being led into the space where I was confined. Two of the people were speaking emphatically to the third.

"You are the only one within miles who deals in small ponies. She doesn't like the white one we bought . . . she said he wasn't the pony she dreamed about. And you do, too, have another . . . right there!" The man pointed to me and the woman nodded.

The third person, evidently the owner of the ponies in the pen and on the track, looked a bit dazed. I began to understand. A moment before, he had owned no white ponies at all. Now he had two, one that the people had returned, and the other myself, just fresh from the Forest Subliminal, and looking my best, if I do say so.

"Well . . ." he drawled. I could see that he was thinking quickly. Not an easy thing for him, I suspected. "I suppose I can make you a deal. Take the cost of Whitey there off the cost of this one. You can see for yourselves he's a much better animal than the other one. More breeding. More intelligence. He almost looks as if he understands what we are saying. Will that suit you?"

"How much more will it be?" asked the woman. She looked at her husband with worried eyes.

The pony man adjusted his figures with lightning speed. "Ten bucks more. Not a bad deal at all. How about it?"

The woman relaxed. Her husband nodded, his expression brightening with relief.

"We'll take him. We have the horse trailer, still, and we can take him right home before we return it to the rental people. Thank you."

As I rode in solitary splendor behind the oldish car, I

mused on the situation. These two (I had managed to hear the man calling them Mr. and Mrs. Allison) were terribly worried about something. That something had to be the child who hadn't liked the first white pony. My client was their child, I was sure. The child who had lost the desire to live . . . the thought made me sad.

They unloaded me onto a sloping drive, where the cement hurt my hooves. But Mrs. Allison led me into a grassy garden, while her husband took away the horse trailer.

"Here, pony. You'll live out here. There's the woodshed, where you can sleep. There's already hay there. And here is Carlie's window. Put your head right up to the screen, will you?" She tugged at my lead, and I managed to turn my head so as to avoid poking a hole with my horn. I got one eye focused to look in.

The room wasn't big. There was a tumbled bed, in which a small figure was wound up in sheets and coverlets until it looked like a cocoon . . . or a mummy. I snorted delicately, whiffling my nostrils.

The cocoon jerked and wriggled. A round face came into view, and the whole wad sat upright, thrusting away the covers. A little girl, about ten years old, was staring at me as if she had waited all her life for one glimpse of me.

"A unicorn!" she breathed, and I saw that she was one of the very few of humankind who could see us as we are, no matter how magically we may be disguised.

Beside me, her mother laughed. "Not quite, dear. But it is another white pony. Does this one suit you?"

The child didn't note the anxiety in the woman's voice, but I did. Carlie was struggling across the bed to put her face up against the screen of the window.

I could see that she was terribly weak. She dragged her legs behind her, pulling herself along with her arms. Her hair was lackluster, and her eyes, even temporarily bright with surprise, lacked something vital.

"Snow!" she said, still softly, as if she had too little strength to speak loudly. "Snow . . . my unicorn!"

The woman patted my shoulder. I could feel her gratitude in her touch. She said to the child, "Lie down again, dear. I'll feed Snow some grain, and then your father will be home. I am making soufflé for supper."

The child lay down, but I noted that the mention of food drew no response. That told me a lot. We may spend our age-long lives sporting in the forests and lingering after maidens, but we unicorns study the human animal closely. I understood Carlie, now, as well as the pain in her parents' eyes.

The shed was comfortable, though no Forest Subliminal, of course. The grain was acceptable, and I had a nice view of the wood bordering the back of the neat farmhouse. Beyond the fence on one side was a nice grassy space, just right for a paddock. I would be more comfortable than I had thought.

"Caroline!" That was the man's voice. He was back.

"Harold? I'm in the kitchen. Carlie . . . Carlie likes the pony!"

The relief in their voices, as they talked, was pleasant to me. Even with the acute hearing of my kind, I couldn't hear their words, but I could tell by their tones that they were joyful.

From time to time I went to the window and gazed in at Carlie. She lay on her smoothed-up bed, staring back at me. A book with a unicorn on the cover lay on her pillow . . . sometimes longing to see us gives a few . . . very few . . . people the ability to do just that. She was one of the lucky ones.

"Do pretend that I am a pony," I whispered to her.

"Grown-ups don't believe in unicorns, and you will upset them."

Her eyes widened. Then she nodded. "It will be our secret?"

"Our secret," I replied. "Mum's the word?"

Her nod, this time, was more feeble. I could see blue veins in her throat and at her wrists. Something had to be done, very soon, or this child was going to waste away quietly and sadly. For no reason, really, except discouragement and despair. I knew why I had been sent so quickly.

"Tomorrow," I said to Carlie, "you can ride on my back."

Her eyes, very blue, widened even more. "I can't sit up!" she protested.

"You sat up just a while ago, when I looked into your window. Straight, too, as if you had a poker up your back."

She frowned. "I did, didn't I? But mostly I'm too tired to sit up. Do you truly think I'll be able to ride you? Ever?"

I gazed at her thoughtfully. Tomorrow would be rushing it a bit. But with a good appetite to fill her body with energy and an incentive . . . I thought she very well might.

"Perhaps not tomorrow, but I suspect that we will soon be exploring together. Set your mind on that, why don't you? Eat and rest, and then we shall see what happens."

"I rest all the time. And it's too much trouble to eat," she grumbled. She looked at me as if I should be able to wave my horn and fix everything instantly.

It just doesn't work that way, though there are things I could do to help. I dipped my head, and the tip of my horn poked a tiny hole in the screen.

"We'll add a bit of magic . . . put your finger up and rub the tip of my horn . . . right there. Rub it round and round, to make the magic come off."

She obeyed my instructions, and the tingle that contact brought made me understand why my kind took such pleasure in helping hers. I took away the horn from the screen and focused an eye on her.

"When your mother brings your supper, flavor it with that magic finger. I guarantee everything will taste super-delicious."

It seemed to work beautifully. I ambled about, pretending to browse on privet bushes and a young lilac, while Caroline brought the child's supper. She propped her daughter up and laid a tray on the girl's lap.

There was a tiny vase with two pink rosebuds on one corner of the tray. A golden soufflé steamed on a hot plate, and beside it were a crisp salad and a glass of milk. Carlie stared down at the tray, then up at me. Tentatively, she touched the plate, the glass, the salad plate with her magic finger. Then she picked up her fork.

I moved closer to the window and chomped loudly. There's nothing like company when you eat.

Carlie didn't look out, but I could see a grin curl her mouth, between bites. Several times she touched her plate again, and every time she seemed to eat with more appetite. Most of the food disappeared quickly.

Caroline stared out into the twilight. She evidently saw my shape against the darkness, for she said, "I believe that your pony has already done you good, dear. Would you like some ice cream?"

I whinnied softly.

She was a quick-witted child. She nodded. "Just a little," she said.

When her light went out, I retired to the shed to think. She had eaten well, and that was a good beginning. I had to come up with enough ploys to keep her eating and moving about and getting ready to rejoin the world she had so nearly left.

It wasn't as easy as it had seemed at first. Though she ate

pretty well, after that first night, her small body had become used to failing slowly. It isn't easy to turn one around when it has decided to die.

I stood by her window, day after day, describing to her the things we would see if we rode together into the wood beyond the fence. Bobolinks swung in the trees, guarding their nests, I told her. Primroses dotted the aisles between the trees. Terrapins trundled busily about their business, and butterflies were beginning to come forth from their cocoons to see the world for a few brief days.

She listened. And over the weeks she began moving about, sitting up for hours, then walking about the house, and at last coming into the yard where I grazed.

One evening, when her father had returned from his work, he lifted her onto my back. It was a strange sensation . . . unicorns were not made for riding, and I had never had a human being on my back before. Yet I found it delightful. This was the goal that had kept her at the attempt to get better.

We took a cautious turn about the garden. She sat straight, her small heels tucked under my belly. I could feel her excitement through the blanket on my back.

When Harold lifted her down again, I knew that she was going to make it. The feeling was far more satisfactory than having flowers braided into my mane, believe me, and mentally I thanked my elder for choosing me for this task.

As Carlie grew stronger, I found to my astonishment that she grew more and more demanding. For all my study of the human creature, I had never really believed that they could be so irrational. I had known the term "spoiled," but I had never before seen it in actuality.

One morning as we moved around the garden, where her mother was weeding the vegetables, I said, "Carlie, you are almost well. We need to begin planning what you will do

. . . you'll be going back to school. You'll begin helping your parents on the farm. There are so many things you are going to be able to do that you haven't done in a long time."

I could feel her astonishment in the tension of her body on my back. She had thought this petted life was to go on forever, I suspected.

"Why?" Her tone was strange.

I choked on the bit in my mouth, which was a terrible thing to try to talk around. Trust the child to go right to the heart of the matter.

I didn't have a ready answer. I could have told her, of course, but children seldom do what they are told and even less often do they believe what their elders tell them . . . even when that elder is a unicorn.

I tried something else. "I was young once," I said. "I lived in a beautiful glade in the Forest Subliminal with my mother, who was strong and beautiful and extremely wise. I was just the sort of silly young colt that goes kicking its heels up, snorting with joy, and never understanding that the world holds many things, some of which are danger and sadness and trouble."

"Even for unicorns?" she asked. Her tone was dubious.

"Even for unicorns. We know perils that human beings cannot dream of, even in their nightmares. My mother knew that, and she was determined that I must learn it." I sighed, for even now the memory was painful.

"She took me into the deepest, darkest part of the Forest Subliminal. There live the terrors that sometimes break loose to stalk even the Temporal World. She led me into a black glade, where even the flowers were brown and gray, and she said to me, 'Stay here. Until you have learned to be independent of me, to think for yourself, to disregard your own pain and fear, you will be no unicorn.' And she left me there."

"How cruel!" said Carlie.

"It would have been more cruel not to do it," I replied. "For I stayed there, though I longed to flee. I stood my ground, and I learned that a fear you will not allow to enter your heart is a fear that cannot harm you. I learned that my mother would not always be there to protect me, so I must learn to protect myself. When she returned for me, I was a unicorn, instead of a thoughtless colt."

There was a long pause. "My parents won't leave me!" said Carlie. "Nobody will ever leave me. I don't want to grow up!"

"You almost didn't," I observed. "Would you have liked that?"

She went silent. I felt her shiver. She had felt the chilly touch of death, in her illness, and suddenly she recalled it.

"People do leave. I will, myself." The moment I said that I knew that the time was near. The last gift I could offer her was the knowledge that all things must end. I stopped beside the porch and allowed her to dismount.

She dropped onto the scrubbed boards and came around to stare into my face, gently rubbing my invisible horn. "You will go?" She sounded close to tears. "No! You can't go!"

"I must," I said. "Soon. And that is not a bad thing but a good one. Once I have gone, you will be on your way to growing up as I would want you to . . . independent and disciplined and brave."

Her hand stroked my horn harder, seeming to fondle the air. "But I'll never see you again!"

"Oh, I wouldn't say that. Some mortals make their way to the Forest Subliminal, from time to time. That is where you will find me, if you are one of those. A long time from now, when you are old and tired of the Temporal World, you may well look for me there."

She turned away to hide her tears. I turned away to hide mine. Our next days together were touched with sadness for us both, and when the last day dawned, we both knew it.

We stood together in the grassy yard for the last time. She rubbed my horn hard, making enough magic rub off to last for a very long time.

I lowered my head, making it easy for her, as her small hands cupped about my nose. She kissed me, very gently.

I sighed. It was time to go. I backed away from her, and her hands dropped to her sides. She smiled, though tears streamed down her cheeks.

"Good-bye. Take care of yourself. Take care of your parents . . . they will need that, you know, someday," I said.

She looked surprised. Then understanding came into her expression. "I will. Good-bye, Snow. Oh, good-bye!"

I went through the hedge and emerged into the glade in the Forest Subliminal. My elder was waiting for my report, and when I was through, he was pleased.

I was pleased, myself.

These days I find maidens who braid flowers into my mane a bit dull. I hope that another summons comes soon . . . I find that I have become addicted to human beings.

WHAT NEWS THE EAGLE BROUGHT

from *The Last Battle*

by *C. S. LEWIS*

The Last Battle *is the final volume of* The Chronicles of Narnia—*seven of the most interesting and exciting fantasies ever written. In this book a clever but wicked ape named Shift finds an old lion skin. He drapes it over Puzzle, a simple, sweet-natured donkey, and fast talks him into pretending to be the great lion Aslan. By showing Puzzle only at night, Shift soon fools Narnia's Talking Beasts into believing the charade.*

Before long, the ape is plotting to take over the whole country. He is helped by Narnia's ancient enemies, the Calormenes, who worship a fearsome god called Tash.

When King Tirian and his best friend, Jewel the Unicorn, try to expose the ape's lies, they are taken captive. All might be lost, if not for the unexpected arrival of Jill Pole and Eustace Scrubb, two earth children brought to Narnia in this hour of need.

Jill and Eustace free Tirian. Then, disguised as Calormenes, they help him rescue both Jewel and Puzzle. Next the group frees a band of dwarfs. But only one, named Poggin, will join their cause. The others, angry at being fooled by the ape, disappear into the hills.

Then, as if things weren't bad enough already, Shift's

wicked lie that Tash and Aslan are one and the same sud-
denly calls a new evil into Narnia.
Which is where this selection begins . . .

It had been sunny when they sat down. Now Puzzle shivered. Jewel shifted his head uneasily. Jill looked up.

"It's clouding over," she said.

"And it's so cold," said Puzzle.

"Cold enough, by the Lion!" said Tirian, blowing on his
hands. "And faugh! What foul smell is this?"

"Phew!" gasped Eustace. "It's like something dead. Is
there a dead bird somewhere bout? And why didn't we
notice it before?"

With a great upheaval, Jewel scrambled to his feet and
pointed with his horn.

"Look!" he cried. "Look at it! Look, look!"

Then all six of them saw; and over all their faces came an
expression of uttermost dismay.

In the shadow of the trees on the far side of the clearing
something was moving. It was gliding very slowly Northward. At first glance, you might have mistaken it for smoke,
for it was gray and you could see things through it. But the
deathly smell was not the smell of smoke. Also, this thing
kept its shape instead of billowing and curling as smoke
would have done. It was roughly the shape of a man but it
had the head of a bird; some bird of prey with a cool, curved
beak. It had four arms which it held high above its head,
stretching them out Northward as if it wanted to snatch all
Narnia in its grip; and its fingers—all twenty of them—were
curved like its beak and had long, pointed, bird-like claws

instead of nails. It floated on the grass instead of walking, and the grass seemed to wither beneath it.

After one look at it Puzzle gave a screaming bray and darted into the tower. And Jill (who was no coward, as you know) hid her face in her hands to shut out the sight of it. The others watched it for perhaps a minute, until it streamed away into the thicker trees on their right and disappeared. Then the sun came out again, and the birds once more began to sing.

Everyone started breathing properly again and moved. They had all been still as statues while it was in sight.

"What was it?" said Eustace in a whisper.

"I have seen it once before," said Tirian. "But that time it was carved in stone and overlaid with gold and had solid diamonds for eyes. It was when I was no older than thou, and had gone as a guest to the Tisroc's court in Tashbaan. He took me into the great temple of Tash. There I saw it, carved above the altar."

"Then that—that thing—was Tash?" said Eustace.

But instead of answering him Tirian slipped his arm behind Jill's shoulders and said, "How is it with you, Lady?"

"A-all right," said Jill, taking her hands away from her pale face and trying to smile. "I'm all right. It only made me feel a little sick for a moment."

"It seems, then," said the Unicorn, "that there is a real Tash, after all."

"Yes," said the Dwarf. "And this fool of an Ape, who didn't believe in Tash, will get more than he bargained for! He called for Tash: Tash has come."

"Where has it—he—the Thing—gone to?" said Jill.

"North into the heart of Narnia," said Tirian. "It has come to dwell among us. They have called it and it has come."

"Ho, ho, ho!" chuckled the Dwarf, rubbing its hairy hands

together. "It will be a surprise for the Ape. People shouldn't call for demons unless they really mean what they say."

"Who knows if Tash will be visible to the Ape?" said Jewel.

"Where has Puzzle got to?" said Eustace.

They all shouted out Puzzle's name and Jill went round to the other side of the Tower to see if he had gone there. They were quite tired of looking for him when at last his large gray head peered cautiously out of the doorway and he said, "Has it gone away?" And when at last they got him to come out, he was shivering the way a dog shivers before a thunderstorm.

"I see now," said Puzzle, "that I really have been a very bad donkey. I ought never to have listened to Shift. I never thought things like this would begin to happen."

"If you'd spent less time saying you weren't clever and more time being as clever as you could—" began Eustace, but Jill interrupted him.

"Oh leave poor old Puzzle alone," she said. "It was all a mistake; wasn't it, Puzzle dear?" And she kissed him on the nose.

Though rather shaken by what they had seen, the whole party now sat down again and went on with their talk.

Jewel had little to tell them. While he was a prisoner he had spent nearly all his time tied up at the back of the Stable, and had of course heard none of the enemies' plans. He had been kicked (he'd done some kicking back too) and beaten and threatened with death unless he would say that he believed it was Aslan who was brought out and shown to them by firelight every night. In fact he was going to be executed this very morning if he had not been rescued.

The question they had to decide was whether they would go to Stable Hill again that night, show Puzzle to the Narnians and try to make them see how they had been tricked, or whether they should steal away eastward to meet the help which Roonwit the Centaur was bringing up from Cair Paravel and return against the Ape and his Calormenes in force. Tirian would very much like to have followed the first plan: he hated the idea of leaving the Ape to bully his people one moment longer than need be. On the other hand, the way the Dwarfs had behaved last night was a warning. Apparently one couldn't be sure how people would take it even if he showed them Puzzle. And there were the Calormene soldiers to be reckoned with. Poggin thought there were about thirty of them. Tirian felt sure that if the Narnians all rallied to his side, he and Jewel and the children and Poggin (Puzzle didn't count for much) would have a good chance of beating them. But how if half the Narnians—including all the Dwarfs—just sat and looked on? Or even fought against him? The risk was too great. And there was, too, the cloudy shape of Tash. What might it do?

And then, as Poggin pointed out, there was no harm in leaving the Ape to deal with his own difficulties for a day or two. He would have no Puzzle to bring out and show now. It wasn't easy to see what story he could make up to explain that. If the Beasts asked night after night to see Aslan, and no Aslan was brought out, surely even the simplest of them would get suspicious.

In the end they all agreed that the best thing was to go off and try to meet Roonwit.

As soon as they had decided this, it was wonderful how much more cheerful everyone became. I don't honestly think that this was because any of them was afraid of a fight (except perhaps Jill and Eustace). But I daresay that each of them, deep down inside, was very glad not to go any nearer —or not yet—to that horrible bird-headed thing which, visible or invisible, was now probably haunting Stable Hill.

Anyway, one always feels better when one has made up one's mind.

Tirian said they had better remove their disguises, as they didn't want to be mistaken for Calormenes and perhaps attacked by any loyal Narnians they might meet. The Dwarf made up a horrid-looking mess of ashes from the hearth and grease out of the jar of grease which was kept for rubbing on swords and spearheads. Then they took off their Calormene armor and went down to the stream. The nasty mixture made a lather just like soft soap: it was a pleasant, homely sight to see Tirian and the two children kneeling beside the water and scrubbing the backs of their necks or puffing and blowing as they splashed the lather off. Then they went back to the Tower with red, shiny faces, looking like people who have been given an extra-specially good wash before a party. They rearmed themselves in true Narnian style with straight swords and three-cornered shields. "Body of me," said Tirian. "That is better. I feel a true man again."

Puzzle begged very hard to have the lion skin taken off him. He said it was too hot and the way it was rucked up on his back was uncomfortable: also, it made him look so silly. But they told him he would have to wear it a bit longer, for they still wanted to show him in that get-up to the other Beasts, even though they were now going to meet Roonwit first.

What was left of the pigeon meat and rabbit meat was not worth bringing away but they took some biscuits. Then Tirian locked the door of the Tower and that was the end of their stay there.

It was a little after two in the afternoon when they set out, and it was the first really warm day of that spring. The young leaves seemed to be much further out than yesterday: the snowdrops were over, but they saw several primroses. The sunlight slanted through the trees, birds sang, and always (though usually out of sight) there was the noise of running water. It was hard to think of horrible things like Tash. The children felt, "This is really Narnia at last." Even Tirian's heart grew lighter as he walked ahead of them, humming an old Narnian marching song which had the refrain:

Ho, rumble, rumble, rumble, rumble,
Rumble drum belaboured.

After the King came Eustace and Poggin the Dwarf. Poggin was telling Eustace the names of all the Narnian trees, birds and plants which he didn't know already. Sometimes Eustace would tell him about English ones.

After them came Puzzle, and after him Jill and Jewel, walking very close together. Jill had, as you might say, quite fallen in love with the Unicorn. She thought—and she wasn't far wrong—that he was the shiningest, delicatest, most graceful animal she had ever met: and he was so gentle and soft of speech that, if you hadn't known, you would hardly have believed how fierce and terrible he could be in battle.

"Oh, this *is* nice!" said Jill. "Just walking along like this. I wish there could be more of *this* sort of adventure. It's a pity there's always so much happening in Narnia."

But the Unicorn explained to her that she was quite mistaken. He said that the Sons and Daughters of Adam and Eve were brought out of their own strange world into Narnia only at times when Narnia was stirred and upset, but she mustn't think it was always like that. In between their visits there were hundreds and thousands of years when peaceful King followed peaceful King till you could hardly remember their names or count their numbers, and there was really hardly anything to put into the History Books. And he went on to talk of old Queens and heroes whom she had never heard of. He spoke of Swanwhite the Queen who had lived before the days of the White Witch and the Great Winter, who was so beautiful that when she looked into any forest pool the reflection of her face shone out of the water like a star by night for a year and a day afterward. He spoke of Moonwood the Hare, who had such ears that he could sit by Caldron Pool under the Thunder of the great waterfall and hear what men spoke in whispers at Cair Paravel. He told how King Gale, who was ninth in descent from Frank the first of all Kings, had sailed far away into the eastern seas and delivered the Lone Islanders from a dragon and how, in return, they had given him the Lone Islands to be part of the royal lands of Narnia forever. He talked of whole centuries in which all Narnia was so happy that notable dances and feasts, or at most tournaments, were the only thing that could be remembered, and every day and week had been better than the last. And as he went on, the picture of all those happy years, all the thousands of them, piled up in Jill's mind like looking down from a high hill onto a rich, lovely plain full of woods and waters and cornfields, which spread away and away till it got thin and misty from distance. And she said:

"Oh, I do hope we can soon settle the Ape and get back to those good, ordinary times. And then I hope they'll go on forever and ever and ever. *Our* world is going to end some day. Perhaps this one won't. Oh, Jewel—wouldn't it be lovely if Narnia just went on and on—like what you said it has been?"

"Nay, sister," answered Jewel, "all worlds draw to an end; except Aslan's own country."

"Well, at least," said Jill, "I hope the end of this one is millions of millions of millions of years away— hullo! what are we stopping for?"

The King and Eustace and the Dwarf were all staring up

at the sky. Jill shuddered, remembering what horrors they had seen already. But it was nothing of that sort this time. It was small, and looked black against the blue.

"I dare swear," said the Unicorn, "from its flight, that it is a Talking bird."

"So think I," said the King. "But is it a friend, or a spy of the Ape's?"

"To me, Sire," said the Dwarf, "it has a look of Farsight the Eagle."

"Ought we to hide under the trees!" said Eustace.

"Nay," said Tirian, "best stand still as rocks. He would see us for certain if we moved."

"Look! He wheels, he has seen us already," said Jewel. "He is coming down in wide circles."

"Arrow on string, Lady," said Tirian to Jill. "But by no means shoot till I bid you. He may be a friend."

If one had known what was going to happen next, it would have been a treat to watch the grace and ease with which the huge bird glided down. He alighted on a rocky crag a few feet from Tirian, bowed his crested head and said in his strange eagle's voice, "Hail, King."

"Hail, Farsight," said Tirian. "And since you call me King, I may well believe you are not a follower of the Ape and his false Aslan. I am glad of your coming."

"Sire," said the Eagle, "when you have heard my news you will be sorrier at my coming than of the greatest woe that ever befell you."

Tirian's heart seemed to stop beating at these words, but he set his teeth and said, "Tell on."

"Two sights have I seen," said Farsight. "One was Cair Paravel filled with dead Narnians and living Calormenes: the Tisroc's banner advanced upon your royal battlements: and your subjects flying from the city—this way and that, into the woods. Cair Paravel was taken from the sea.

Twenty great ships of Calormen put in there in the dark of the night before last night."

No one could speak.

"And the other sight, five leagues nearer than Cair Paravel, was Roonwit the Centaur lying dead with a Calormene arrow in his side. I was with him in his last hour and he gave me this message to Your Majesty: to remember that all worlds draw to an end and that noble death is a treasure which no one is too poor to buy."

"So," said the King, after a long silence, "Narnia is no more."

Whether Narnia really is no more is a complicated question. For the answer, you will have to turn to the pages of The Last Battle.

UNICORN

All that lives of legendry,
Beauty, magic, mystery,
Gentleness and purity,
Dwells in me.

I no mate, no kin, have known;
None may claim me as his own;
One is one, and all alone,
It must be.

Through their weariness and woe
Men have sometimes seen me go,
Felt a wind from Eden blow
Suddenly:

Though they hunt with spear and horn,
Knowing life cannot be borne
If they have no unicorn—
I am free.

Though they kill, and weep to see
Beauty's symbol ended be—
One is one and lives in me
To eternity.

Nicholas Stuart Gray

THE PRINCESS, THE CAT, AND THE UNICORN

by PATRICIA C. WREDE

Princess Elyssa and her sisters lived in the tiny, comfortable kingdom of Oslett, where nothing ever seemed to go quite the way it was supposed to. The castle garden grew splendid dandelions, but refused to produce either columbine or deadly nightshade. The magic carpet had a bad case of moths and the King's prized seven-league boots only went five-and-a-half leagues at a step (six leagues, with a good tail wind).

There were, of course, compensations. None of the fairies lived close enough to come to the Princesses' christenings (though they were all most carefully invited) so there were no evil enchantments laid on any of the three Princesses. The King's second wife was neither a wicked witch nor an ogress, but a plump, motherly woman who was very fond of her stepdaughters. And the only giant in the neighborhood was a kind and elderly Frost Giant who was always invited to the castle during the hottest part of the summer (his presence cooled things off wonderfully, and he rather liked being useful).

The King's councillors, however, complained bitterly about the situation. They felt it was beneath their dignity to run a kingdom where nothing ever behaved quite as it should. They grumbled about the moths and dandelions, muttered about the five-and-a-half-league boots and remonstrated with the Queen and the three Princesses about their duties.

Elyssa was the middle Princess, and as far as the King's councillors were concerned she was the most unsatisfactory of all. Her hair was not black, like her elder sister Orand's, nor a golden corn color, like her younger sister Dacia's. Elyssa's hair was mouse-brown. Her eyes were brown, too, and her chin was the sort usually described as "determined." She was also rather short, and she had a distressing tendency to freckle.

"It's all very well for a middle Princess to be ordinary," the chief of the King's councillors told her in exasperation. "But this is going too far!"

"It was only the second-best teapot," said Elyssa, who had just broken it. "And I did say I was sorry."

"If you'd only pay more attention to your duties, things like this wouldn't happen!" the councillor huffed.

"I dusted under the throne just this morning," said Elyssa indignantly. "And it's Orand's turn to polish the crown!"

"I don't mean those duties!" the councillor snapped. "I mean the duties of your position. For instance, you and Orand ought to be fearfully jealous of Dacia, but are you? No! You won't even try."

"I should think not!" Elyssa said. "Why on earth should I be jealous of Dacia?"

"She's beautiful and accomplished and your father's favorite, and—and elder Princesses are *supposed* to dislike their younger sisters," the councillor said.

"No one could dislike Dacia," Elyssa said. "And besides, Papa wouldn't like it."

The councillor sighed, for this was undoubtedly true. "Couldn't you and Orand steal a magic ring from her?" he pleaded. "Just for form's sake?"

"Absolutely not," Elyssa said firmly, and left to get a broom to sweep up the remains of the teapot.

But the councillors refused to give up. They badgered and pestered and hounded poor Elyssa until she simply could not bear it anymore. Finally she went to her stepmother, the Queen, and complained.

"Hmmph," said the Queen. "They're being ridiculous, as usual. I could have your father talk to them, if you wish."

"It won't do any good," Elyssa said.

"You're probably right," the Queen agreed, and they sat for a moment in gloomy silence.

"I wish I could just run off to seek my fortune," Elyssa said with a sigh.

Her stepmother straightened up suddenly. "Of course! The very thing. Why didn't I think of that?"

"But I'm the *middle* Princess," Elyssa said. "It's youngest Princesses who go off to seek their fortunes."

"You've been listening to those councillors too much," the Queen said. "They won't like it, of course, but that will be good for them." The Queen was not at all fond of the councillors, because they kept trying to persuade her to turn her stepdaughters into swans or throw them out of the castle while the King was away.

"It would be fun to try," Elyssa said in a wistful tone. She had always liked the idea of running off to seek her fortune, even if most of the stories did make it sound rather uncomfortable.

"It's the perfect solution," the Queen assured her. "I'll arrange with your father to leave the East Gate unlocked tomorrow night, so you can get out. Orand and Dacia can help you pack. And I'll write you a reference to Queen Hildegard from two kingdoms over, so you'll be able to find a nice job as a kitchen maid. We won't tell the councillors a thing until after you've left."

To Elyssa's surprise, the entire Royal Family was positively enthusiastic about the scheme. Orand and Dacia had a long, happy argument about just what Elyssa ought to carry in her little bundle. The King kissed her cheek and told her she was a good girl and he hoped she would give the councillors one in the eye. And the Queen offered Elyssa the magic ring she had worn when *she* was a girl going off on adventures. (The ring turned out to have been swallowed by the castle cat, so Elyssa didn't get to take it with her after all. Still, as she told her stepmother, it was the thought that counted.) All in all, by the time Elyssa slipped out of the postern door and set off into the darkness, she was downright happy to be getting away.

As she tiptoed across the drawbridge, Elyssa stepped on something that gave a loud yowl. Hastily, she pulled her foot back and crouched down, hoping none of the councillors had heard. She could just make out the shape of the castle cat, staring at her with glowing, reproachful eyes.

"Shhhh," she said. "Poor puss! Shhh. It's all right."

"It is not all right," said the cat crossly. "How would you like to have your tail stepped on?"

"I don't have a tail," Elyssa said, considerably startled. "And if you hadn't been lying in front of me, I wouldn't have stepped on you."

"Cat's privilege," said the cat, and began furiously washing his injured tail.

"Well, I'm very sorry," Elyssa said. "But I really must be going." She stood up and picked up her bundle again.

"I don't know how you expect to get anywhere when you can't see where you're going," said the cat.

"I certainly won't get anywhere if I stay here waiting for the sun to come up," Elyssa said sharply. "Or do you have some other suggestion?"

"You could carry me on your shoulder, and I could tell

you which way to go," the cat replied. "*I* can see in the dark," he added smugly.

"All right," Elyssa said, and the cat jumped up on her shoulder.

"That way, Princess," the cat said, and Elyssa started walking.

"How is it you can talk?" she asked, as she picked her way carefully through the darkness according to the cat's directions. "You never did before."

"I think it was that ring of your mother's I swallowed yesterday," the cat said. He sounded uneasy and uncomfortable, as if he really didn't want to discuss the matter. So, having been well brought up, Elyssa changed the subject. They chatted comfortably about the castle cooks and the King's councillors as they walked, and periodically the cat would pat Elyssa's cheek with one velvet paw and tell her to turn this way or that way. Finally the cat announced that they had come far enough for one night, and they settled down to sleep in a little hollow.

When she awoke next morning, the first thing Elyssa noticed were the trees. They were huge; the smallest branches she could see were three times the size of her waist, and she couldn't begin to reach around the trunks themselves. The ground was covered with green, spongy moss, and the little flowers growing out of it looked like faces. Elyssa glanced around for the cat. He was sitting in a patch of sunlight with his tail curled around his front paws, staring at her.

"This is the Enchanted Forest, isn't it?" she said accusingly.

"Right the first time, Princess," said the cat.

Elyssa frowned. She knew enough about the Enchanted Forest to be very uncomfortable about wandering around in it. It lay a little to the east of the kingdom of Oslett, and the castle had permanently mislaid at least two milkmaids and a woodcutter's son who had carelessly wandered too far in that direction. The Enchanted Forest was one of those places that is very easy to get into, but very hard to get out of again.

"But I was supposed to go to Queen Hildegard!" Elyssa said at last.

"You wouldn't have liked Hildegard at all," the cat said seriously. "She's fat and bossy, and she has a bad-tempered, unattractive daughter to provide for. She'd be worse than the King's chief councillor, in fact."

"I don't believe you," Elyssa said. "Stepmama wouldn't send me to a person like that."

"Your stepmother hasn't seen Queen Hildegard since they were at school together twenty-some years ago," said the cat. "You're much better off here. Believe me, I know."

Elyssa was very annoyed, but it was much too late to do anything about the situation. So she picked up her bundle and set off in search of something to eat, leaving the cat to wash his back. After a little while, Elyssa found a bush with dark green leaves and bright purple berries. The berries looked very good, despite their unusual color, and she leaned forward to pick a few for breakfast.

"Don't do that, Princess," said the cat.

"Where did you come from?" Elyssa demanded crossly.

"I followed you," the cat answered. "And I wouldn't eat any of those berries, if I were you. They'll turn you into a rabbit."

Elyssa hastily dropped the berry she was holding and wiped her hand on her skirt. "Thank you for warning me," she said. "I don't suppose you know of anything around here that I *can* eat? Or at least drink? I'm very thirsty."

"As a matter of fact, there's a pool over this way," said the cat. "Follow me."

The cat led her through the trees in a winding route that Elyssa was sure would bring them right back to where they had started. She was about to say as much when she came around the bole of a tree into a moss-lined hollow. Green light filtered through the canopy of leaves onto the dark moss. In the center of the hollow, a ring of star-shaped white flowers surrounded a still, silent, mirror-dark pool of crystal-clear water.

"How lovely!" Elyssa whispered.

"I thought you were thirsty," said the cat. His tail twitched nervously as he spoke.

"I am," Elyssa said. "But—oh, never mind." She knelt down beside the pool and scooped up a little of the water in her cupped hands.

"Who steals the water from the unicorn's pool?" demanded a voice like chiming bells.

Elyssa started, spilling the water down the front of her dress. "Drat!" she said. "Now look what you've made me do!"

As she spoke, she looked up, expecting to see the person who had spoken. There was no one there, but the chiming voice spoke again, in stern accents. "Who steals the water from the unicorn's pool?"

Elyssa wiped her hands on the dry portion of her skirt and cast a reproachful look at the cat. "I am Elyssa, Princess of Oslett, and I'm very thirsty," she said in her best royal voice. "So if you don't mind—"

"A Princess?" said the chiming voice. "Really! Well, it's about time. Let me get a look at you."

A breath of air, scented with violets and cinnamon, touched Elyssa's face. An instant later, a unicorn stepped delicately out of the woods. It halted on the other side of the pool and stood poised, its head raised to display the sharp, shining ivory horn, its mane flowing in perfect waves along its neck. Its eyes shone like sapphires, and its coat made Elyssa think of the white silk her stepmother was saving for Dacia's wedding dress.

"Gracious!" Elyssa said.

"Yes, I am, aren't I?" said the unicorn complacently. It lowered its head slightly and studied Elyssa. An expression very like dismay came into its sapphire eyes. *"You're* a Princess? Are you quite sure?"

"Of course I'm sure," Elyssa replied, nettled. "I'm the second daughter of King Callwil of Oslett; ask anybody. Ask him." She waved at the cat.

The unicorn scowled. "I should hope I would never need to ask a cat for anything," it said loftily.

"Overgrown, stuck-up goat," muttered the cat.

"What did you say?" demanded the unicorn.

"Nothing that would interest you," said the cat.

"You may go, then," the unicorn said grandly.

"I'm quite happy right here," the cat said. "Or I was until you came stomping in with your silly questions."

"How dare— Princess Elyssa! What are you doing?" said the unicorn.

Elyssa took a last gulp of water and let the rest dribble through her fingers and back into the pool. "Having a drink," she said. She really *had* been very thirsty, and she had taken advantage of the argument between the cat and the unicorn to scoop up another handful of water.

"Well, I suppose it's all right, since you're a Princess," the unicorn said. Its chiming voice sounded positively sulky.

"Thank you," said Elyssa. She stood up and shook droplets from her fingers. "It's very good water."

"Of course it's good water!" the unicorn said. "A unicorn's pool is always pure and sweet and crystal clear and—"

"Yes, yes," said the cat. "But it's time we were going. Princess Elyssa has to seek her fortune, you know."

"Leave?" said the unicorn. It lifted its head in a regal gesture, and light flashed on the point of its horn. "Oh no, you can't leave. Not the Princess, anyway."

"What?" Elyssa said, considerably taken aback. "Why not?"

"Why, because you're a Princess and I'm a unicorn," the unicorn said.

"I don't see what that has to do with anything," Elyssa said.

"You will gather trefoils and buttercups and pinks for me, and plait them into garlands for my neck," the unicorn went on dreamily, as if Elyssa hadn't said anything at all. "I will rest my head in your lap, and you will polish my horn and comb my mane."

"Sounds like an exciting life," said the cat.

"Your mane doesn't need combing," Elyssa told the unicorn crossly. "And your horn doesn't need polishing. As for flowers, I'll be happy to have Stepmama send you some dandelions from the garden at home. But I'm not interested in staying here for goodness knows how long just to plait them into garlands."

"Nonsense," said the unicorn. "You're a Princess. All Princesses adore unicorns."

"Well, I don't," Elyssa said firmly. "And I'm not staying."

The cat lashed his tail in agreement, and gave the unicorn a dark look.

"You don't have a choice," the unicorn said calmly. "You're not much of a Princess, but you're better than nothing, and I'm not letting you go. I've been stuck out here on the far edge of the Enchanted Forest for years and years, with no one to sing songs about me or appreciate my beauty, and I deserve some consideration."

"Not from me, you don't," Elyssa muttered. She decided that the cat had been right to call the unicorn a stuck-up goat. "I'm sorry, but we really must leave," she said in a louder tone. "Good-bye, unicorn." She picked up her bundle and started for the edge of the hollow.

The unicorn watched with glittering eyes, but it made no move to stop her. "I don't like this," the cat said as he and Elyssa left the hollow.

"You're the one who found that pool in the first place," Elyssa pointed out.

The cat ducked its head. "I know," he said uncomfortably. "But—"

He broke off abruptly as they came around one of the huge trees and found themselves at the edge of the hollow once more. The unicorn was watching them with a smug, sardonic expression from the other side of the pool.

"We must have gotten turned around in the woods," Elyssa said doubtfully.

The cat did not reply. They turned and started into the woods again. This time they walked very slowly, to be certain they did not go in a circle. In a few minutes, they were back at the hollow.

"Had enough?" said the unicorn.

"Third time lucky," said the cat. "Come on, Princess."

They turned their backs on the unicorn and walked into the woods. Elyssa concentrated very hard, and kept a careful eye on the trees.

"I think we're going to make it this time," she said after a little. "Cat? Cat, where are—oh, dear." She was standing at the edge of the hollow, looking across the pool at the unicorn.

"The cat is gone for good," the unicorn informed her in a satisfied tone.

Elyssa felt a pang of worry about her friend. "What did you do to him?" she demanded.

"I got rid of him," the unicorn said. "I don't want a cat; I want a Princess. Someone to comb my mane, and polish my horn—"

"—and make you garlands, I know," Elyssa said. "Well, I won't do it."

"No?" said the unicorn.

"No," Elyssa said firmly. "So you might as well just let me go."

"I don't think so," the unicorn said. "You'll change your mind after a while, you'll see. I'm much too beautiful to resist. And I expect that with a little work you'll improve a great deal."

"Elyssa doesn't need your kind of improvement," said the cat's voice from just above Elyssa's head.

Elyssa looked up. The cat was perched in the lowest fork of the enormous tree beside her. "You came back!" she said.

"Did you really think I wouldn't, Princess?" said the cat. "I'd have gotten here sooner, but I wanted to make sure of the way out. Just in case you've had enough of our conceited friend."

"You're bluffing, cat," said the unicorn. "Princess Elyssa can't get out unless I let her, and I won't."

"That's what you think," said the cat. "Shall we go, Princess?"

"Yes, *please*," said Elyssa.

"Put your hand on my back, then, and don't let go," said the cat.

Elyssa bent over and put her hand on the cat's back, just below his neck. It was a very awkward and uncomfortable way to walk, and she was sure she looked quite silly. She had to concentrate very hard to keep from falling or tripping and losing her hold as she sidled along. "How much farther?" she asked after what seemed a long time.

"Not far," said the cat. Elyssa thought he sounded tired. A few moments later they entered a large clearing (which contained neither a pool nor a unicorn), and the cat stopped. "All right, Princess," the cat said. "You can let go now."

Elyssa took her hand off the cat's back and straightened up. It felt very good to stretch again. When she looked down, the cat was lowering himself to the ground in a stiff and clumsy fashion that was quite unlike his usual grace.

"Oh, dear," said Elyssa. She dropped to her knees beside the cat and stroked his fur, very gently. "Are you all right, cat?" she asked, because she couldn't think of anything else to say.

The cat did not answer. Elyssa remembered all the stories she had ever heard about animals who had been gravely injured or even killed getting their masters or mistresses out of trouble, and she began to be very much afraid. "Please be all right, cat," she said, and leaned over and kissed him on the nose.

The air shimmered, and then it rippled, and then it exploded into brightness right in front of Elyssa's eyes. She blinked. An exceedingly handsome man dressed in brown velvet lay sprawled on the moss in front of her, right where the cat had been.

Elyssa blinked again. The man propped his head on one elbow and looked up at her. "Very nice, Princess," he said. "But I wouldn't mind if you tried again a little lower down."

"You're the cat, aren't you?" Elyssa said.

"I was," the man admitted. He sat up and smiled at her. "You don't object to the change, do you?"

"No," said Elyssa. "But who are you now, please?"

"Prince Riddle of Amonhill," the man said. He bowed to her even though he was still sitting down, which proved he was a Prince. "I made the mistake of stopping at Queen Hildegard's castle some time ago, and she changed me into a cat when I refused to marry her dreadful daughter."

"Queen Hildegard? But I was supposed to go see her!" Elyssa exclaimed.

"I know. I told you you wouldn't like her," Prince Riddle said. "She condemned me to be a cat until I was kissed by a Princess who had drunk the water from a unicorn's pool. Her daughter was the only Princess the Queen knew of who had tasted the water. If she had also managed to kiss me I'd have had to marry her." He shuddered.

"I see," said Elyssa slowly. "So that's why you brought me to the Enchanted Forest and then found the unicorn's pool."

Riddle looked a little shamefaced. "Yes. I didn't expect to have any trouble with the unicorn; they usually aren't around much. I'm sorry."

"It's quite all right," Elyssa said hastily. "It was very interesting. And I'm glad I could help you. And—and you don't need to think that you have to marry me just because I disenchanted you."

"It *is* traditional, you know," Riddle said, with a sidelong glance that reminded Elyssa very strongly of the cat.

"Well, I think it's a silly tradition!" Elyssa said in an emphatic tone. "What if you didn't like the Princess who broke the spell?"

Riddle smiled warmly. "But I do like you, Princess."

"Oh," said Elyssa.

"You were always very nice to me when I was a cat."

"Yes," said Elyssa.

"And I like the idea of marrying you." Riddle looked at her a little uncertainly. "That is, if you wouldn't mind marrying me."

"Actually," said Elyssa, "I'd like it very much."

So Elyssa and Riddle went back to the castle to be married. Elyssa's family was delighted. Her papa kissed her cheek and clapped Riddle on the back. Her stepmama cried with joy and then was happily scandalized to hear about the doings of her old school friend Queen Hildegard. And both of Elyssa's sisters agreed to be bridesmaids (much to the dismay of the King's councillors, who felt that it was bad enough for a middle Princess to be married first without emphasizing the fact by having her sisters stand up for her).

The wedding was a grand affair, with all the neighboring Kings and Queens in attendance. There were even a couple of fairies present, which made the King's councillors more cross than ever. (Fairies, according to the chief councillor, were supposed to come to christenings, not to weddings.) After the wedding, Elyssa had her stepmama send a special note to Queen Hildegard. A few days later, Queen Hildegard's daughter disappeared into the Enchanted Forest, and shortly thereafter rumors began circulating that the unicorn had found a handmaiden even more conceited than it was.

And so they all lived happily for the rest of their lives, except the King's councillors, who never would stop trying to make things go the way they thought things ought to be.

STARHORN

Run, Starhorn
Carry fire leaping from your starhorn
    Pierce worlds
    Cleft suns
    Tangle clouds
    Shatter time
        With your flaming starhorn
Bring a wish, a maiden's wish
    Head in lap
    Eyes soft
        Starhorn.

Shirley Rousseau Murphy

THE COURT OF THE SUMMER KING

by JENNIFER ROBERSON

The wind was a wolf. It came slinking, trotting, running—*leaping* out of the night, finally, to tear at the throat of the encampment as a real wolf tears at the throat of a deer.

Winter was always the worst of the Mother's seasons, Asta knew. No matter how hard the clan worked to store enough provisions for the long cold months when the Mother of the Earth and the Sky and the World turned her face away to tend her other children, the time was never easy. Asta had forgotten how many nights since babyhood she and Gar had huddled together beneath the bearskins to share one another's warmth, fearing there would come a time when the Mother might forget to look back on *them* again, denying them summer forever.

Summer, when the World was warm and the clan basked in the light of her love.

The winter wolf howled, and blew, and plucked icy claws at the seams and lacings of the tent pegged so firmly into the hardened ground. Asta had no fear the wolf-wind would actually find a way in, because her father and mother had worked too hard to make the tent wind- and water-tight. But she disliked the solitude. She disliked the wailing of the wolf, echoing the sounds she had heard issuing too often this winter from human mouths.

The keening, grieving wails that meant another of the Mother's sons or daughters had been taken by the fever.

And Elki— No. She put away the thought at once. To think of Elki was to voice the fear, to give in to it, to unlace the door flap and invite the winter wolf inside.

And yet it was so hard *not* to think of Elki, little Elki, the newborn sister only four weeks old. Winter-born, Elki was hardly strong enough to fight off the fever that ravaged the clan. Even now she was in the care of the healer, whose skills were already so much in demand by others of the clan.

She heard a voice calling her name above the wail of the winter wolf, and Asta hastened to unlace the flap of the tent. It was Gar, buried beneath leather and fur, who ducked inside in a flurry of sleet and quickly hunched down by the fire.

Gar coughed, but she knew that cough. It was a sound all of them made, clearing the wolf from their throats. Asta watched as Gar shed heavy furs and leathers and scooped the hood back from his head, baring a face so very much like her own. It should be; they were twins. As alike in dark hair, dark eyes and ruddy skin as in temperament, which was to say both of them had known frequent lectures from their parents for being too bold, too glib, too rash. For being too reckless when care was necessary.

Gar's face looked old to her, too old for fifteen. There were worry lines etched in his flesh. "The healer will keep her the night."

Asta sighed a little as relief temporarily rushed in to wash away the dread. At least Elki wasn't dead. "They'll stay too?" She meant their parents.

"They'll stay. But—" Gar broke it off, lips pressed together. She knew what he wanted to say, and wouldn't; to speak even in passing reference of a death before it occurred ensured the winter wolf a meal.

"Oh, by the Mother, I wish there was something we could do!" Asta cried, clenching hands into fists of rage. "I feel so *helpless* like this, cocooned out of the wind while the clan dwindles away to nothing, stolen by this fever!"

Gar's face was troubled. "It may be there *is* something."

"*What?*" Asta leaned forward on her knees.

"There is—a name." Gar's face was solemn. Melting sleet dripped from the hair framing his face, edges the hood had not warded adequately against the winter wolf. "Rahela."

Rahela. Asta said it silently, within her mind, knowing better than to speak the witch's name aloud. Although no one really knew in what way the witch's power manifested itself, or how much she really claimed, they *did* know enough to be very careful when speaking or thinking about her. One could never be sure.

"Rahela," Gar said. "Come morning."

But Asta saw beneath the firmness in his tone to the worry and the fear.

The wind died at dawn. The wolf was silenced for the day, perhaps the week—if they were lucky, the Mother would chase him away for good. But it was unlikely, Asta thought, slogging through snow. There was nothing of spring in the air. It was cold, bitter cold, and the sun gazed only fitfully through folds in the World's winter cloak.

Asta's exhalations fogged the air. Ahead of her, breathing like a bellows, Gar broke a trail. He kicked ruffles of snow into her path, but it was easier than breaking it by herself.

Rahela's tent, like all of them, was a small domed mushroom shape, pegged down against snow and wind. But it sat apart from the others, huddled like a single sentinel in a tight-grown copse of trees. A thread of bluish smoke wove its way from the opened vent to the naked branches of the trees, where it tangled briefly, then rose again to smudge the dull gray sky. Asta smelled the pungent tang of cedar, mixed with oak.

A dog came running, and then another. Big dogs, both, and ferocious in their barking.

In answer, the woman ducked out of the tent. Like Gar and Asta, she was wrapped against the weather—shapeless, weighted, made faceless in the gray shadows of the day. She whistled the dogs away.

The children stopped just short of the woman. Now her face was clear. Asta saw it was not so much different from her own: ruddy, angular, planed down from winter's limited rations. The eyes were a familiar dark brown, as were the lashes and eyebrows. But there was a bit of silver in her hair, to match the fine netting of lines etched into the skin around her eyes and mouth.

"Your names," Rahela said quietly.

Asta slanted a sideways glance at Gar. They both knew telling a true name to a witch gave her special power over that person.

But this was for Elki, still too young to know her own.

"Asta," she said softly, and heard the tremor in her voice.

Gar hesitated a moment longer. Then the single syllable of his name spilled out on a rush of breath.

Rahela smiled a little, and some of the lines went out of her face even as newer ones came in. "Now you may enter, Gar and Asta. But be wary of the little ones."

Rahela's tent was smaller than their own. But it needed to be larger, Asta thought, as she ducked inside behind Gar and sat down on layers of pelts. Everywhere she looked there were animals. The two dogs, panting by the fire. Cats and nursing kittens, tangled like skeins of yarn. Even a

ferret and a fox kit. It was no wonder Rahela burned cedar. The tent smelled of musk and fur.

But also of herbs and roots and spices, and other magical things.

Rahela pulled the flap down as she entered, then moved to kneel down across from them. Almost at once one of the cats untangled herself from nursing kittens and sprawled across Rahela's lap as the witch put aside her blanket. One slim, tough hand began to stroke the tabby's fur, and Asta heard the muted purr.

"Well?" Rahela asked. "Were you sent, or did you come?"

"We—came," Gar said. "Is it permitted?"

"Permitted, oh yes." Rahela sighed a little. "Welcomed, also. I am too often alone. But that is the price *I* pay." Dark eyes flicked suddenly to Asta. "What price are *you* willing to pay for the spell you want from me?"

Asta drew in a breath. "For Elki," she said, and then nearly gasped aloud in alarm. Now the witch knew Elki's name as well.

"Our sister." It was Gar's turn. "Just a month old, and sick from the fever like so many others."

For only a moment, Rahela's hand stopped stroking the cat. And then it began again. *"That* is why you have come."

"For the fever, yes," Asta nodded. "Have you a spell? Isn't there anything you can give us to ward Elki from the fever? A charm? Perhaps a medicine tea?"

Rahela stared into the fire. She continued to stroke the cat. "I have none of those things." Her voice was oddly flat.

"But you are a *witch!"* In his urgency, Gar leaned forward. One of the dogs growled until Rahela spoke a word. "Can't you give us something?"

"For your needs, I have none of those things." Rahela's brow was furrowed as if she fought a private pain. "I know this fever too well. I have seen it before, once. It came as the winter wolf, and lived with us the season, until the Mother turned her face to us again. And then it was gone, as quickly as it had come. But it took many of us with it. Many of us died. My husband. My parents. My children. And I was left alone."

Asta stared at Rahela. She had not known a witch could cry.

"Is there nothing?" whispered Gar. "I would give anything—"

"Would you give your life?" Rahela's voice was steady. "To save the life of your small sister, who might die anyway in the hardships of the Mother's winter, you waste yet another life? Maybe two?" Her eyes included his twin. "For Elki, you offer Gar and Asta?"

Gar's face was white. "Then—that is your price? Our lives?"

"Not *my* price," Rahela declared. "By the Mother, not mine. But I won't lie to you and say there is no risk."

"Then you *do* know a way," Asta said intently.

"I have learned many things since turning to the magic," Rahela said quietly. "One of these things is that every sickness has a cure. But the cure may itself be dangerous to find, or may demand great sacrifice. Often it is impossible to find at all, or"—she paused a moment, then finished very softly —"or impossible to *win.*"

Gar frowned. "What do you mean?"

Rahela's face was very serious. In that moment she seemed both old and young, wiser than even the healer and the headman. Certainly wise enough to know what they faced in their quest to save their sister.

Abruptly, the witch made up her mind. With quick, deft movements she brought out a brass tripod and a silver bowl, wrapped carefully in soft deerskin beaded with rune-signs. Rahela set the tripod before her, by the fire, then rested the silver bowl in the curving upright prongs. From a hide-wrapped jug she poured water into the bowl, up to the rune-worked rim, then put the jug away. Chanting beneath her breath, Rahela closed her eyes and made signs in the air with nimble fingers, tracing invisible patterns. Then, still chanting softly, she touched one forefinger to the surface of the water and set the bowl afire.

As one, Asta and Gar recoiled. But they did not flee. Transfixed, they sat very still on folded legs and stared at the silver bowl, where flame danced on water even though such a thing was impossible.

Rahela put her hand, palm-down, over the bowl. Flame licked at flesh, but she did not give any indication it burned. Slowly she lowered the hand until it covered the bowl from rim to rim, and the flame was snuffed out. The smoke showed briefly gold, then silver, then bronze, and was gone.

"Now," she said softly, "you may see where you must go to win this thing: the Court of the Summer King."

Asta slowly crept up to the bowl balanced on its gleaming tripod. Gar knelt beside her, and they stared at the water that was no longer water, but a window to the World.

Asta drew in a breath of wonder. *"Unicorns,"* she whispered.

Rahela nodded. "The most beautiful of all the Mother's children."

Gar frowned. "What have unicorns to do with a cure for the fever?"

"A unicorn's horn is the most powerful, magical thing known in the Mother's World," Rahela said simply. "Win one, and you will have the means to cure the entire clan as well as Elki. Probably forever."

Gar stared at the witch. "If you knew that, why haven't you told the headman? Why haven't you told the healer? Why tell *us?"*

"Because you asked," Rahela answered. "Your need was greater." Her dark eyes, full of distances, were on Asta. "And because not just anyone may find a unicorn. It takes a very special person. A young woman, like your sister." Briefly there was a glint of tears in her eyes. "I might have tried myself, except it was too late for me. I had a husband. Children. But Asta might be the one."

"What can *I* do?" Asta asked, astonished.

"You can win the unicorn's trust," Rahela said. "How else can you win the horn?"

Crossly, Gar shook his head. "We don't even know how to *find* a unicorn. And even if we did, why worry about *winning* the horn? Even you said our need was greater—why can't we just *take* it?"

"It would not be difficult to *take* one, as you say, from a colt or filly." Rahela kept her voice toneless. "The horns of the young are fragile and easily broken, and even a fragment would be enough for your needs—" She stopped, as if reluctant to speak, then continued very quietly. "But to take even a little, without consent, would kill the unicorn."

"Oh," Asta said in dismay. "Oh *no.*"

Even Gar seemed taken aback. But his grim expression renewed itself. "Asta—it's for Elki. Remember?" He fixed an unwavering stare on Rahela. "How do we find a unicorn?"

She touched a finger to the surface of the water and banished the Court of the Summer King. In silence they watched as she took a small leather pouch from a chest and loosened the drawstrings. From it she took two objects, an ivory needle polished glossy white, and a long silver thread, tensile as wire.

Rahela threaded the needle and knotted it. Before Asta could speak, she caught the girl's right hand and held it out, palm upright, looping the thread over her middle finger. The needle dangled limply, pointing to the ground.

"When it moves," the witch said, "follow it. When it dances, you have found the proper place."

"But—" Gar began.

"Go." Rahela looked at Asta. "It is a true diviner, that I promise you. It will lead you to the Court of the Summer King."

Asta nodded. Carefully, she put needle and thread back into the pouch and tucked it away within the folds of her woolen tunic, buried beneath furs and leathers. "Thank you," she said softly. Tugging at Gar's furs to urge him outside, Asta ducked out of the tiny tent so full of magic and animals.

They stood near the river some distance from the encampment. The morning was gone, spent in futile attempts to make the needle indicate the proper way. So far, it hadn't stirred a bit.

"How many more times?" Gar asked, exasperated. "I think the witch lied. I think this needle and thread is nonsense."

"I don't." Steadfastly, Asta held out her arm. The needle hung motionless. "She said it was a true diviner. We just haven't found the right place yet."

"Elki could die while we stand out here waiting for nothing," Gar muttered.

Asta's hand clenched the silver thread. "Don't say that, Gar! You know better!"

"It's the truth. She might. So might we all, witch or no witch." Gar bent, dug a stone from the snow, threw it with all his might toward the river. It fell into frigid, slushy water with a thunking splash.

Troubled, Asta looked at the polished needle. In silence she begged it to do something, *anything,* if only to prove her brother wrong. Somehow, she trusted Rahela. She trusted the diviner to do precisely what Rahela had said it would do. She *had* to believe; it was the only thing left to her. It was better than feeling helpless.

And then, as Asta turned to look again at her brother, the needle began to move. "Gar!"

It trembled. Stirred. Twitched. Finally, in a slow, steady revolution, the needle began to *seek.*

"Look," Asta breathed.

"You're doing that."

"No . . . no, I'm not. Oh, Gar—it's *working!"*

He came up close to her, but Asta didn't even bother to look at him. She stared at the needle in fascination, tongue caught between teeth, begging it to show her the proper way.

At last, it stopped moving. The polished tip pointed north.

"There," Asta said, and began to walk steadily.

Gar followed after a moment. "But—you don't know where it's taking you!"

"To the Court of the Summer King." Asta, grinning, didn't take her eyes off the pointing needle. "Just as Rahela said."

They walked. Always north. Asta lost track of how far they had gone, though Gar occasionally muttered something about turning back before it was too late. But he didn't. He just followed along like a tame but suspicious dog, intent on learning the secret of the unicorn diviner.

"Wait! Oh, Gar—*look!"*

He looked. The needle, suspended on its thread, spun and

spun, until the thread was wrapped tight as yarn on a spindle. Then it unwrapped, spinning in the opposite direction, until the thread was smooth as silk again and the needle was pointing at a massive old oak, half-shattered by a lightning blast that had split the trunk nearly in two. A huge charred cleft marred the frost-rimmed trunk.

"Asta—"

She didn't listen. She merely followed the line of the needle to the charred cleft. Putting out a hand to touch it, she touched nothingness instead.

Nothingness.

And it swallowed her whole, leaving emptiness in her place.

Asta tumbled out of the Mother's harshest season into Her gentlest. In place of snow there was grass, lush, thick grass, green as the World's summer cloak. The warm bright face of the Mother's sun touched all the World with gold. Asta, still clutching the silver thread, stared speechlessly at a world that was so much like her own, and realized it *was* her own. Only the seasons had altered.

"Summer," she breathed aloud, and then from behind her she heard Gar's garbled outcry as he tumbled out of the cleft.

"Asta . . . *Asta—*"

"I know," she said sternly. "Hush, Gar—we are in the Court of the Summer King."

"That's *nonsense—*" But Gar was silenced, because before them stood the proof: a unicorn in the flesh.

Not the Summer King himself, whom Asta had seen in the bowl. Much younger, smaller, with his pride intact but less pronounced. Mostly, he seemed curious. Long-lashed, amber-honey eyes peered quizzically from under a pale gold forelock that fell between two erect, cream-colored ears tufted impishly at the tips, and dusted with only the faintest sheen of brilliant gold. The soft rosy-gold muzzle quivered a moment. Whiskers shimmered, tipped with droplets of sun-gilded dew. Nostrils expanded widely, inhaled noisily, then snorted, as if in surprise.

"The horn," Gar said intently.

It was smaller than Asta had expected. Its fragile root was hidden within silky layers of shining forelock, and suddenly she realized the silver thread she held wasn't thread at all, but a strand of hair from the mane or tail of a unicorn. The horn matched the young unicorn's wide-spaced, astonished eyes—amber and honey and gold. It twisted from root to tip in a lazy, symmetrical spiral.

"If I grab his head"—Gar began—"*you* can grab the horn—"

"No." Asta's tone was final. Slowly, carefully, so as not to frighten the unicorn, she put away the diviner. Then, hands outstretched, she took a step toward the colt.

He eyed her curiously, showing no fear. Delicate amber hooves barely depressed the flowers and grass beneath the tree. He was not a horse, and certainly not a riding animal, but with enough similarities that Asta longed to stroke his velvet muzzle, to tangle her hands in his shining mane, to feel the sleek, glossy back beneath her as she galloped across the meadows of the Court of the Summer King.

"The horn," Gar hissed distinctly.

Asta felt warm, soft breath as the unicorn cradled his muzzle in her palms. She smelled the scent of flowers and the tang of spice in the air, a clean, fresh scent unlike any she had known. She felt the vibration of the colt's exhalations against her fingers and saw the winding spiral of the glossy horn as it jutted from his brow, parting the shining forelock that swept down to brush her wrists with a subtle seductiveness.

Eyes half-shut, the unicorn rested his jaw upon her shoulder.

It would be so easy, she knew. One twist, one *snap!* of the fragile horn—

"Do it *now,*" Gar whispered.

But Asta knew she could not.

"For *Elki,*" Gar urged. "For Elki and the clan!"

Asta cupped her palms against the colt's neck and stroked the glossy cream-pale hair, as Rahela had stroked her cat. There was warmth in the flesh beneath the hair, and life and strength and health. She tangled fingers in his mane and knew her soul was tangled as well, trapped within the web of unicorn magic.

Whose trust was won, she wondered? The unicorn's or her own?

"Asta!" Gar hissed. "Get the horn and let's *go—*"

For Elki— Asta bit her bottom lip. *Just grab it and twist—* Inwardly, she shuddered. "No." She said it mostly to the colt, whose head was not so much higher than her own. "I can't."

"But you *have* to . . ." Gar's voice was insistent. "Not for me, not for you—for Elki. For the clan. It's what we came to do."

"I know. I *know.*" Asta shut her eyes and buried her face in the silk of the unicorn's mane. "But surely the Mother wouldn't want me to *kill* one of her children merely to save another."

And abruptly, even as Asta finished speaking, the unicorn shed his shape and became a woman instead.

The Mother's smile was the light of the World. Her eyes and nails were of gold, the yellow-gold of a summer sun, and her gown was spun of spider silk and delicate, gilt-bright flowers. The hair flowing down her back was amber and honey and gold.

Gar fell to his knees. Asta stood locked in silence.

"Rahela chose well," the Mother said, and her voice was the song of a summer rain, cool and soft and sweet.

Gar trembled. "But—it was for *Elki.* Our sister. She's only a baby, only a little one . . . we had to do *something*—"He rubbed gloved hands nervously on his fur-lined leathers. "She's just a *baby*—"

"I know," the Mother said. "I know all things. I know that even now the winter wolf howls on the hilltops, singing his song of death. But you are here, not there, and so there is something to be done before I send you back."

"Must you?" Asta looked at the bright vale of summer-glow, the Court of the Summer King. "Even if I wanted to stay here?"

The Mother shook her head and her radiance increased. "All my children have their places. You are out of yours. If the World is to turn again, you must go back before the day is done."

Asta drew in a breath. "We came for the unicorn's horn."

"But you did not take it."

"No." Asta looked at the ground. "I couldn't."

The Mother's laughter was the lilt of a meadowlark's song. And then it stopped. "You still may," she said. "I will give you a choice, because that is the way I made the World. There are choices in everything." Her hand was on Asta's head, smoothing bark-brown hair. Gold nails shed dancing sparks of brass-bright sunlight. "I consent to the sacrifice. Take the horn. Go back to your clan. Save Elki and the others. You will never know fever again."

"Or?" Asta asked.

"Or go back with nothing and take the chance that Elki will survive."

Gar scrambled to his feet. "Asta—*do* it. Take the horn, just to be sure."

"With your consent . . ." Asta looked into the Mother's blinding eyes. "What is the price, if I do?"

The hand fell away from her head and took the sunlight with it. "Never to know summer again."

Asta stared. "Never?"

"No." The Mother shrugged. "But winter need not be deadly. Your clan would learn to survive."

"Asta," Gar began.

"It is your choice," the Mother told Asta. "You must decide."

Outraged, Asta shook her head. "I *can't!* How can you expect me to save Elki and the others, but only so they must learn what it is to live forever in winter? Mother, I think you are too cruel."

"Too cruel, too kind. Mothers must often be so, when dealing with their children." Behind the woman, unicorns gamboled in the vale. The Summer King with his golden horn was ablaze in brilliant sunlight. "You must decide, Asta."

Asta shut her eyes. Behind her lids she could still see the unicorns, horns agleam in the sunlight. So *alive* in the summer warmth.

She opened her eyes. "Send us back," Asta said. "Mother, send us back. Even for Elki, I can't sentence the others to summerless lives. In the end, it would kill us all. In spirit, if not in body."

The Mother smiled. Her hair was a summer sunset; her eyes the dawn of the coming day. "Rahela chose well indeed."

"So," Gar said curtly, "we go home with *nothing.*"

Asta held her silence, knowing he was weary and worried and frightened of what they would find when they went back, just as she herself was. Resolutely she turned to look at the Mother, only to fall back a step. "Gar—*look!*"

It was the young unicorn yet again, honey-gold eyes agleam as he stepped daintily through grass and flowers to set his head against Asta's shoulder. He rubbed, grunting, and Asta braced herself on spread legs before he could knock her down. Head bowed, the colt rubbed repeatedly, knocking the horn gently against the top of her shoulder, until the root itself crumbled away in a shower of powdered gold.

Asta caught the horn as it fell. It was warm and smooth to the touch, so silky, with its perfectly symmetrical spiral. In shock, she stared at it in her hands, and then she looked at the colt.

He seemed almost to sigh, as if glad to be rid of the burden. He shook his head and the forelock parted, just enough to expose the nub of a newborn horn. The horn of an adult. Its tip was purest gold.

Gar's laugh was a short bark of sound. "So all of it was meaningless, all that nonsense about choices . . . the Mother *tricked* you, Asta! Don't you see? A unicorn is no different from a deer. It *shed* its horn, Asta, like a puppy shedding milk-teeth!"

"Meaningless?" She shook her head. "I don't think so. He *gave* it to us, Gar. *He* consented for us to have it, not the Mother for him. We won the unicorn's trust, and so we won the horn. Just as Rahela said."

For the last time Asta tangled her hands in his silken mane, still clutching the gleaming horn, and set her face against his neck. She breathed in the tangy spice of his scent, gloried in the texture of his coat, was touched by the magnitude of his trust. And then, in silence, she thanked him, and turned back again to the tree.

Gar's frown indicated the depth of his worry for her, and his bafflement.

Asta blinked tears away. "Don't you see, Gar? There are

choices in everything . . . things that can be freely given, but can't be *taken* without a price. Without a sacrifice."

"Asta—"

"Come on, Gar," she said gently, "let's go home. Let's go home to Elki. When summer comes, we can teach her how to swim."

And with the horn clutched in her hand, Asta slipped back through the tree into the world she knew again, where the winter wolf howled on the hilltops, impatient for summer to come.

THE STRANGERS

Early this morning,
    About the break of day,
Hoofbeats came clashing
    Along the narrow way—-

And I looked from my window
    And saw in the square
Four white unicorns
    Stepping pair by pair.

Dappled and clouded,
    So daintily they trod
On small hooves of ivory
    Silver-shod.

Tameless but gentle,
    Wondering yet wise,
They stared from their silver-lashed
    Sea-blue eyes.

The street was empty
    And blind with dawn—
The shutters were fastened,
    The bolts were drawn,

And sleepers half-rousing
    Said with a sigh,
"There goes the milk,"
    As the hooves went by!

Audrey Alexandra Brown

THE BOY WHO DREW UNICORNS

by JANE YOLEN

There was once a boy who drew unicorns. Even before he knew their names, he caught them mane and hoof and horn on his paper. And they were white beasts and gray, black beasts and brown, galloping across the brown supermarket bags. He didn't know what to call them at first, but he knew what they called him: Phillip, a lover of horses, Philly, Phil.

Now, children, there is going to be a new boy in class today. His name is Philadelphia Carew.

Philadelphia? That's a city name not a kid's name.

Hey, my name is New York.

Call me Chicago.

I got a cousin named India, does that count?

Enough, children. This young man is very special. You must try to be kind to him. He'll be very shy. And he's had a lot of family problems.

I got family problems too, Ms. Wynne. I got a brother and he's a big *problem.*

Joseph, that's enough.

He's six feet tall. That's a very *big problem.*

Now you may all think you have problems, but this young man has more than most. You see, he doesn't talk.

Not ever?

No. Not now. Not for several years. That's close enough to ever, I think.

Bet you'd like it if we didn't talk. Not for several years.
No, I wouldn't like that at all, though if I could shut you
up for several hours, Joseph . . .
Oooooh, Joey, she's got you!

"What is the good of such drawing, Philadelphia?" his
mother said. "If you have to draw, draw something useful.
Draw me some money or some groceries or a new man, one
who doesn't beat us. Draw us some better clothes or a bed
for yourself. Draw me a job."

But he drew only unicorns: horse-like, goat-like, deer-
like, lamb-like, bull-like, things he had seen in books. Four-
footed, silken swift, with the single golden horn. His corner
of the apartment was papered with them.

When's he coming, Ms. Wynne?
Today. After lunch.
Does he look weird, too?
He's not weird, Joseph. He's special. And I expect you—all
of you—to act special.
She means we shouldn't talk.
No, Joseph, I mean you need to think before you talk.
Think what it must be like not to be able to express yourself.
I'd use my hands.
Does he use his hands, Ms. Wynne?
I don't know.
Stupid, only deaf people do that. Is he deaf?
No.
Is there something wrong with his tongue?
No.
Why doesn't he talk, then?
Why do you think?
Maybe he likes being special.
That's a very interesting idea, Joseph.

Maybe he's afraid.
Afraid to talk? Don't be dumb.
Now, Joseph, that's another interesting idea, too. What
are you afraid of, children?
Snakes, Ms. Wynne.
I hate spiders.
I'm not afraid of anything!
Nothing at all, Joseph?
Maybe my big brother. When he's mad.

In school he drew unicorns down the notebook page, next to all his answers. He drew them on his test papers. On the bathroom walls. They needed no signature. Everyone knew he had made them. They were his thumbprints. They were his heartbeats. They were his scars.

Oooooh, he's drawing them things again.
Don't you mess up my *paper, Mr. Philadelphia Carew.*
Leave him alone. He's just a dummy.
Horses don't have horns, dummy.
Here comes Ms. Wynne.
If you children will get back in your seats and stop crowding around Philly. You've all seen him draw unicorns before. Now listen to me, and I mean you, too, Joseph. Fold your hands and lift those shining faces to me. Good. We are going on a field trip this afternoon. Joseph, sit in your seat properly and leave Philly's paper alone. A field trip to Chevril Park. Not now, Joseph, get back in your seat. We will be going after lunch. And *after your spelling test.*
Oooooh, what test, Ms. Wynne?
You didn't say there was going to be a test.

The park was a place of green glades. It had trees shaped like popsicles with the chocolate running down the sides. It had trees like umbrellas that moved mysteriously in the wind. There were hidden ponds and secret streams and moist pathways between, lined with rings of white toadstools and trillium the color of blood. Cooing pigeons walked boldly on the pavement. But in the quiet underbrush hopped little brown birds with white throats. Silent throats.

From far away came a strange, magical song. It sounded like a melody mixed with a gargle, a tune touched by a laugh. It creaked, it hesitated, then it sang again. He had never heard anything like it before.

I hear it, Ms. Wynne. I hear the merry-go-round.
And what does it sound like, children?
It sounds lumpy.
Don't be dumb. It sounds upsy-downsy.
It sounds happy and sad.
Joseph, what do you think it sounds like?
Like another country. Like "The Twilight Zone."
Very good, Joseph. And see, Philly is agreeing with you. And strangely, Joseph, you are right. Merry-go-rounds or carousels are from another country, another world. The first ones were built in France in the late 1700s. The best hand-carved animals still are made in Europe. What kind of animals do you think you'll see on this merry-go-round?
Horses.
Lions.
Tigers.
Camels.
Don't be dumb—camels.
There are too! I been here before. And *elephants.*

He saw unicorns, galloping around and around, a whole herd of them. And now he saw his mistake. They were not like horses or goats or deer or lambs or bulls. They were like —themselves. And with the sun slanting on them from beyond the trees, they were like rainbows, all colors and no colors at all.

Their mouths were open and they were calling. That was the magical song he had heard before. A strange, shimmery kind of cry, not like horses or goats or deer or lambs or bull; more musical, with a strange rise and fall to each phrase.

He tried to count them as they ran past. Seven, fifteen, twenty-one . . . he couldn't contain them all. Sometimes they doubled back and he was forced to count them again. And again. He settled for the fact that it was a herd of unicorns. No. *Herd* was too ordinary a word for what they were. Horses came in herds. And cows. But unicorns—there had to be a special word for them all together. Suddenly he knew what it was, as if they had told him so in their wavery song. He was watching a *surprise* of unicorns.

Look at old weird Philly. He's just staring at the merry-go-round. Come on, Mr. Phildelphia Chicago New York L.A. Carew. Go on up and ride. They won't bite.

Joseph, keep your mouth shut and you might be able to hear something.

What, Ms. Wynne?

You might hear the heart's music, Joseph. That's a lot more interesting than the flapping of one's own mouth.

What does that mean, Ms. Wynne?

It means shut up, Joseph.

Ooooh, she got you, Joey.

It means shut up, Denise, too, I bet.

All of you, mouths shut, ears open. We're going for a ride.

We don't have any money, Ms. Wynne.

That's all taken care of. Everyone pick out a horse or a

whatever. Mr. Frangipanni, the owner of this carousel, can't wait all day.

Dibs on the red horse.

I got the gray elephant.

Mine's the white horse.

No, Joseph, can't you see Philly has already chosen that one.

But heroes always ride the white horse. And he isn't any kind of hero.

Choose another one, Joseph.

Aaaah, Ms. Wynne, that's not fair.

Why not take the white elephant, Joseph. Hannibal, a great hero of history, marched across the high Alps on elephants to capture Rome.

Wow—did he really?

Really, Joseph.

Okay. Where's Rome?

Who knows where Rome is? I bet Mr. Frangipanni does.

Then ask Mr. Frangipanni!

Italy, Ms. Wynne.

Italy is right. Time to mount up. That's it. We're all ready, Mr. Frangipanni.

The white flank scarcely trembled, but he saw it. "Do not be afraid," he thought. "I couldn't ever hurt you." He placed his hand gently on the tremor and it stopped.

Moving up along the length of the velvety beast, he saw the arched neck ahead of him, its blue veins like tiny rivers branching under the angel-hair mane.

One swift leap and he was on its back. The unicorn turned its head to stare at him with its amber eyes. The horn almost touched his knee. He flinched, pulling his knee up close to his chest. The unicorn turned its head back and looked into the distance.

He could feel it move beneath him, the muscles bunching and flattening as it walked. Then with that strange wild cry, the unicorn leaped forward and began to gallop around and around the glade.

He could sense others near him, catching movement out of the corners of his eyes. Leaning down, he clung to the unicorn's mane. They ran through day and into the middle of night till the stars fell like snow behind them. He heard a great singing in his head and heart and he suddenly felt as if the strength of old kings were running in his blood. He threw his head back and laughed aloud.

Boy, am I dizzy.
My elephant was the best.
I had a red pony. Wow, did we fly!
Everyone dismounted? Now, tell me how you felt.

He slid off the silken side, feeling the solid earth beneath his feet. There was a buzz of voices around him, but he ignored them all. Instead, he turned back to the unicorn and walked toward its head. Standing still, he reached up and brought its horn down until the point rested on his chest. The golden whorls were hard and cold beneath his fingers. And if his fingers seemed to tremble ever so slightly, it was no more than how the unicorn's flesh had shuddered once under the fragile shield of its skin.

He stared into the unicorn's eyes, eyes of antique gold so old, he wondered if they had first looked on the garden where the original thrush had sung the first notes from a hand-painted bush.

Taking his right hand off the horn, he sketched a unicorn in the air between them.

As if that were all the permission it needed, the unicorn nodded its head. The horn ripped his light shirt, right over

the heart. He put his left palm over the rip. The right he held out to the unicorn. It nuzzled his hand and its breath was moist and warm.

Look, look at Philly's shirt.
Ooooh, there's blood.
Let me through, children. Thank you, Joseph, for helping him get down. Are you hurt, Philly? Now don't be afraid. Let me see. I could never hurt you. Why, I think there's a cut there. Mr. Frangipanni, come quick. Have you any bandages? The boy is hurt. It's a tiny wound but there's lots of blood so it may be very deep. Does it hurt, dear?

No.

Brave boy. Now be still till Mr. Frangipanni comes.
He spoke, Ms. Wynne. Philly spoke.
Joseph, do be still, I have enough trouble without you . . .
But he spoke, Ms. Wynne. He said "no."
Don't be silly, Joseph.
But he did. He spoke. Didn't you, Philly?
Yes.

Yes.
He turned and looked.
The unicorn nodded its head once and spoke in that high, wavering magical voice. "THE HORN HEALS."
He repeated it.

Yes. The horn heals.
He spoke! He spoke!
I'll just clean this wound, Philly, don't move. Why—

that's strange. There's some blood, but only an old scar. Are
you sure you're all right, dear?
  Yes.

  Yes.
  As he watched, the unicorn dipped its horn to him once,
then whirled away, disappearing into the dappled light of
the trees. He wondered if he would ever capture it right on
paper. It was nothing like the sketches he had drawn before. Nothing. But he would try.

  Yes, Ms. Wynne, an old scar healed. I'm sure.

ABOUT THE AUTHOR

BRUCE COVILLE is an award-winning author of over fifteen books for children, including *Herds of Thunder, Manes of Gold* and *Prehistoric People,* also for Doubleday. "Fantasy at its best" was the phrase *Publishers Weekly* used to describe one of his previous books. Mr. Coville has also contributed to numerous magazines and newspapers, including *Sesame Street Parent's Newsletter* and *Cricket.* Formerly an elementary school teacher, he now writes full-time from his home in New York City.

ABOUT THE ARTIST

TIM HILDEBRANDT is an award-winning artist and illustrator whose work has appeared in countless bestselling books, posters and calendars. After attending Meinzinger's Art School in Detroit, Michigan, Mr. Hildebrandt worked as an animator for ten years before turning to illustration. The artist lives in Gladstone, New Jersey, where he currently divides his time between several book and film projects.